Treasure up in Smoke

DAVID WILLIAMS

Treasure up in Smoke

ST. MARTIN'S PRESS,
NEW YORK

Library of Congress Cataloging in Publication Data

Williams, David, 1926-
　　Treasure up in smoke.

　　I. Title.
PZ4.W72254Ts　[PR6073.I42583]　823'.9'14　78-4010
ISBN 0-312-81648-0

This one for
Linda and Jonathan

CHAPTER I

'One never drops names – as I said to the Prince this morning.' Lord Grenwood intended no witticism. He poked a finger into the hairy orifice of his left ear, examined the result of this exploration with close interest and then continued. 'I see no reason, though, why you shouldn't tell the Governor – what's the chap's name?'

'Rees – Sir Archibald Rees.'

'Archie Rees, that's the fellow. Eton and Christ Church.'

'Brecon and London University,' Mark Treasure corrected firmly, anticipating the momentary expression of displeasure that followed. The venerable Lord Grenwood, Chairman of Grenwood, Phipps and Co., respected Merchant Bankers in the City of London, harboured fixed notions about what he considered a seemly educational provenance for colonial administrators. Treasure, chief executive in the same establishment, but Grenwood's junior by some thirty years, nurtured no such predilections. He was himself the product of a lesser public school and what had been an unfashionable Oxford College; such distinctions had been meaningful at one time.

Lord Grenwood rallied; in view of the general drop in standards, he reflected, there was some compensation in knowing that Her Majesty's representative on King Charles Island had been educated at all. 'Socialist appointment, was it?' he asked, resignation in his tone.

'Tory, actually. He's been there some time. You were saying?'

Grenwood leant forward to press an electric button on his desk. His hand returned to touch the knot of his bow tie. 'Oh yes. No harm in your telling this . . . er . . . Rees –' Archie had been relegated as an impostor – 'we've got more than just a Commonwealth Office blessing on this one.'

'You mean the Royal Family . . .'

The Chairman glanced about him to ensure his office had not been infiltrated by republican spies. 'No need to be too specific, dear boy, but the island does have rather special ties with the monarchy . . .'

'With the House of Stuart,' Treasure interrupted irreverently.

Grenwood chose not to be confused by historical minutiae. 'Suggest – very obliquely, you understand – there could be a peerage in it . . . er, life peerage, of course.' The Grenwood title was hereditary; courtesy of Lloyd George for services and other considerations rendered. 'We're all human, after all.' This last generalization was charitably intended to include graduates of London University, and if this was an unguarded over-indulgence on the part of the speaker, the reason was plainly due to a distraction.

In answer to the electronic summons a well built and loudly attractive young woman had entered and moved with confident steps to where Grenwood was sitting – a relatively considerable distance. Lord Grenwood watched the girl's progress with undivided attention, his straightened frame pushed well to the back of the chair, stomach in.

'Mark, you've met . . . er . . . Dorothy?'

'Deirdre,' the girl corrected: notwithstanding, she had been baptized Ethel.

'Deirdre, of course. This is Mr Treasure, my dear, Vice-Chairman of the Bank.'

Treasure half rose from his seat, nodded and smiled. George Grenwood changed attractive secretaries practically with the seasons and invariably following one of his wife's carefully spaced visits to the office. This connection was obvious, but the reason for it as perceived by even close observers – including Grenwood himself – was invariably wrong. Lady Grenwood was a tolerant and wise woman who believed change and challenge to be the best defence against waning libertarianism and the prospect of her husband retiring – or even coming home too early. He rarely came home late.

'We'd like some coffee, wouldn't we, Mark?' Treasure nodded. 'Oh, make it for three, and ask Mr Peregrine Gore to join us, there's a good girl.' The gaze that accompanied these instructions and lingered on the retreating form of his secretary suggested that goodness might not be the exact virtue Lord Grenwood expected in his new employee. 'What a corker, eh, Mark? Fooled the old girl again.'

Lady Grenwood's only confidant smiled in apparent agreement. 'And you want Peregrine to come with us?'

'Not exactly with you, Mark, no. To go on ahead, I thought, soften the ground; get the locals teed up for you and Molly, as it were. Then he can be your ADC while you tie things together.' Grenwood finished with an especially engaging smile – a sure indication that he felt uncomfortable.

Grenwood, Phipps were acting for an Anglo-Australian consortium bidding for an interest in the West Indian island of King Charles. In financial terms the project was not massive, and in normal circumstances would have been handled by one of the Bank's four Joint Managing Directors – with Treasure exercising a supervisory role from London. It would certainly not have involved Lord Grenwood, nor put Treasure in the situation of having to be instructed by the non-executive Chairman. But the circumstances were not quite normal. The British company involved in the consortium – a client of the Bank's for more than fifty years – was controlled by a chairman nearly as decrepit as Grenwood himself. The two men were old cronies and had enjoyed progressing the proposals in principle – that is, up to the point where the necessity for real application had appeared imminent. That was when Grenwood had grandly promised Treasure's personal involvement.

For his part, Treasure had accepted the obligation with a good grace – the more so when he discovered that his usually busy actress wife would be free to join him on the necessary visit to the island. He was aware that his brief involved out-manœuvring an American hotel group – rival bidders for the business concession available on King Charles Island – but he savoured the prospect of competition. He had personally taken a view on his mission from the Commonwealth Office. The Minister had been predictably enthusiastic about a project aimed at improving the prosperity of a Crown Colony; he had been unspecific about the likelihood of financial backing from the Commonwealth Development Fund (which he controlled), but richly optimistic about the prospect of massive support from the United Nations Development Programme and the Caribbean Development Bank whose available assets were no concern of his.

Treasure was as Royalist as the next man but he doubted the alleged encouragement from Buckingham Palace could be converted into a negotiating tool – always supposing it had been offered at all; Lord Grenwood was given to fantasizing in such matters.

What Treasure found unnerving was the news that his labours in the Caribbean were to be lightened by the presence of Peregrine Gore – though on quick reflection he could find no fair reason to offer for eschewing such aid. Some days later he came to regret not having voiced an unfair one – but by then it was too late.

Certainly the presence of a junior executive would be helpful – but there were a dozen young men in the Bank's employ that Treasure would have chosen before the nominated Gore. It was not that he disliked the boy – Treasure, despite his still dashing good looks, was far enough into early middle-age subconsciously to classify any male under thirty as juvenile. Charitably he considered that Peregrine Gore might even be a good fellow to have beside him in a tight corner – even if he could immediately think of no one more likely to get him into one.

The famous general who had made a similar observation about one of his officers had been spared the witness of Peregrine's shorter than most short-service commissions in the Brigade of Guards. Sound family connections had ensured his safe passage through Sandhurst Military Academy and into a famous Regiment – too famous. It was the chapter of accidents – or near misses – which followed that had prompted the late and face-saving discovery of colour blindness, a handicap which while not incapacitating had been sufficient excuse for honourable retirement with very little seniority. This recourse had been the invention not of an army doctor but of a lieutenant-colonel, who considered that Peregrine's mistaking an off-duty Indian porter on Camberley Station for the important Arab ambassador he had been sent to meet as convenient evidence of serious ocular deficiency.

In mitigation, it ought to be recorded that Peregrine never endangered the lives of his men – even before the time those in authority decided he should not be given further opportunity to do so. He brought a good deal of happiness to many: for instance, the off-duty porter had never ridden in a Daimler before. Changing the guard at St James's Palace twice during the first morning of British Summer Time was a mistake that might have been made by anybody called on duty at short notice before resetting his watch. The soldiers had found a good deal of amusement in this harmless episode: unfortunately it had occurred only a few weeks before the Camberley incident, which in turn had been quickly compounded by the mishap involving the Field Marshal's mistress.

Thus it could be said there were any number of reasons why Peregrine Gore had entered merchant banking. As Treasure watched him sitting alert and upright before Lord Grenwood he wondered again whether he and others had misjudged the chap. Gore had been with the Bank

nearly eighteen months, and while he had not been asked
to shoulder any great responsibility, he applied himself
with enthusiasm and there had been good reports from
some quarters. Only the day before, Wilfred Jonkins,
Assistant Manager of the Trust Department, had described
Peregrine to Treasure as 'a most well-informed young
gentleman'. Jonkins had not specified the particular area
of information on which he had been seeking enlightenment during the month the ex-officer had been assigned
to him for training: it had concerned the construction of
explosive devices. The mild-mannered Jonkins had been
passively planning new ways to liquidate his wife for
more than twenty years: it helped him to sleep.

'It's a splendid opportunity for you, my boy.' Grenwood had been explaining the King Charles assignment
to Peregrine in some detail. 'Mr Treasure here is a hard
task-master, but I'm sure you'll justify the confidence
we're . . . um, we're both placing in you.'

'Oh, absolutely sir.' Peregrine answered Grenwood but
addressed Treasure: he recognized where the confidence
might be weakest. The Vice-Chairman warmed visibly. It
was part of Peregrine's charm that he could inspire too
much trust from people – while still leaving them in no
doubt about his limitations. He turned again to Lord
Grenwood. 'Just one thing, Uncle. Where exactly is
King Charles Island?'

Molly Treasure stood at the sink; she was clad in an
elegant shantung kaftan and pink rubber gloves. Better
known as Margaret Forbes, the deservedly celebrated
actress, she was applying the same seemingly effortless
poise to washing up as she had lavished on her final
performance in the part of Elvira Condomine the night
before at the Queen's Theatre. Noël Coward's *Blithe
Spirit* had been acclaimed as the most charming revival in
the London theatre for many seasons, and Molly a
captivating and marvellously ethereal first Mrs Condomine.

'Then we should get a dishwasher that *does* do knives.'
The Vice-Chairman of Grenwood Phipps was standing at
the draining board, tea-towel at the ready, but not liking
it. There was a fitness in most things, but he found it hard
to make a case for wiping up.

Mr and Mrs Pink, the Treasures' resident chauffeur
and cook, had the night off; so had Molly – the first for
many months. She had elected to prepare dinner at home
herself. 'Nonsense,' she said with characteristic, comic
imperiousness.

Molly had first won a place at acting school by playing
Portia's 'quality of mercy' speech from *The Merchant of
Venice* in the manner of a suburban *grande dame* admonish-
ing the milkman for overcharging. That was eighteen
years ago, and she had sustained her career by producing
elegant variations on that same characterization ever
since – to the delight of theatre and screen audiences on
both sides of the Atlantic.

Tall and striking – more statuesque than beautiful –
Molly was a thoroughbred patrician to the tip of her
aquiline nose, and once admirably described as the
unchallenged mistress of withering heights. Her talent to
amuse by projecting comic disdain, outrage and offended
innocence if it was in a sense limited had kept her in
constant demand – for revivals of Sheridan, Wilde and
Coward, and latterly for stylish new works by Michael
Frayn and William Douglas Home. The scene she was
now playing was the closest she had ever been to a kitchen
sink drama. 'Wiping four knives is as good for your ego as
it is for their handles,' she added.

'*And* an elephantine dish.' Treasure peered into the
receptacle searching for damp.

'Better and better. You didn't call the soufflé elephantine.'

'It was quite edible – like you.' He kissed her on the
neck.

'Oh sir, I'll 'ave to tell the mistress.' Molly emptied the
plastic bowl and began removing the gloves as though in

preparation for taking tea with Lady Bracknell. 'Is Peregrine Gore the good-looking blond one?'

'I suppose so.' After spending half the day with Peregrine on the Caribbean project the young man's appearance was not the characteristic uppermost in Treasure's mind. He bunched the tea-towel and deposited it on the kitchen table 'He's Algy Grenwood's step-son by the second wife.'

'That's much too complicated.' She rescued the towel and arranged it neatly on a hanger. 'I remember him, though. Wasn't he the one who courageously put out the fire at the Phippses' cocktail-party?'

Treasure had no memory of this, but he considered there was a quite logical reason why Peregrine might have been the person closest to the outbreak. 'I don't remember,' he answered truthfully. 'Actually, he's got lots of charm and it'll probably amuse you to have him along . . .'

'While you decide the fate of nations. Why exactly are we going?'

The two ascended the stairs to the living-room of the house in Chelsea's Cheyne Walk – their home for more than a decade.

'You're going because you've promised to take a rest.'

'You mean because I'm out of work, and no one's offered me a play.' Molly seated herself at the piano and began picking out the melody of a Chopin Nocturne.

'A play you want to do,' Treasure corrected. He knew his wife had been more than usually selective about her work in the months ahead so that they could spend more time together. 'What about *The Rivals* in April?'

'That's for TV, it's three months away, and I know the part – which means I only need to unlearn the actions and deftly woo the upstage camera.' She smiled. 'You still haven't told me why I have to behave like a banker's wife for once.'

Treasure was turning the pages of a large atlas. 'We're putting together a simple little deal for King Charles Island. It's so simple even your precious Peregrine understands it – I think. Anyway, it's a Crown Colony, we're staying with the Governor, and since your opportunities for social advancement are so few, I thought . . .'

'I'll have you know I've appeared in more palaces than you, young man,' Molly interrupted in her best Edith Evans voice. 'Including the old Victoria.' She continued playing. 'Incidentally, where exactly is King Charles Island?'

Treasure placed the open atlas on the music stand of the Bechstein. 'Somehow I thought you'd ask that question. It's known colloquially as KCI and it's there.' He placed his finger below the tiny dot on the quite large-scale map.

'Hm. I should have thought Peregrine could have handled that on his own. What shall we do for encores – buy back Long Island?' She broke into the opening bars of 'Rule, Britannia' that make the introduction to 'Mad dogs and Englishmen got out in the midday sun' – a not entirely inappropriate overture for events soon to follow.

CHAPTER II

It would be no more than fairly accurate to say that Columbus discovered what later came to be called King Charles Island on 16 May 1503. He was beating up from Panama towards Hispaniola at the time, and during his fourth visit to the New World. He was behind schedule, well west of where he intended to be, and distinctly *blasé* about the superabundance of hitherto unidentified and boring-looking landfalls attending the voyage. A rough translation of his son's journal runs: 'We did sight a treacherous-seeming island well populated by sea birds and thickly vegetated, the whole at ransom to a towering, vast volcano at the north. We did not tarry.' This somewhat discouraging first review appears to have summed up the attitude of traders and potential settlers alike for well over a century.

Los Pajaros, as the island was called by the Spanish, lies some 150 miles due east of the Caymans, and ninety miles north-west of Jamaica. Shaped a little like a miniature Ireland, it is small – only seven miles north to south, and five miles wide. Strategically it was not considered commanding, its shores were uninviting, it offered little that anyone might want to take away – except fresh water – and for a reason lost in antiquity it acquired the reputation of being the haunt of evil spirits. For all these reasons the Carib Indians who had made the island their home were left to live there undisturbed for quite a long time – in sharp contrast to the fate their race suffered at the hands of European infiltrators practically everywhere else in the Caribbean.

The Caribs acquired their warlike and savage reputation chiefly on account of their excusably warlike and savage attitude to the white usurpers, who found their presence inconvenient and slaughtered them in large numbers. In the ordinary way the Caribs lived sensible, ordered and contented lives. The womenfolk – of legendary beauty – were model wives. It is recorded that they spent most of their time massaging their husbands' bodies, and knitting them hammocks. The men, handsome and fearless, were expert hunters, well versed in the art of camouflage. Independent by nature, they found obedience to superiors intolerable and slavery more so. Clearly, they had to go.

The Caribs who had fetched up on Los Pajaros maintained a perfectly adequate existence from its natural resources – fish, birds and fruit – plus the progeny of some wild boar which had been put ashore by the Spaniards at the time when those compulsive colonists thought it prudent, as it were, in passing, to drop livestock on every island that looked capable of sustaining life. The evil spirits that discouraged proper European settlement were taken in their stride by the Caribs. A logical race, they had never seen the point of worshipping the provider of all things bright and beautiful. Instead they made sacrifices to Manitou, the source of all things dark and nasty, beseeching him not to be horrid to them. In this they were some way ahead of European scepticism which, two centuries later, questioned the credibility of a deity that created evil as well as good. True to form, the Caribs gave the name Manitou to the volcano that dominated their home – and so it is still known today.

When a certain Michael O'Hara and party landed on the south-east corner of Los Pajaros in the January of 1652 they were met by hails of arrows and a well-practised display of fearsome mumbo-jumbo intended to strike terror in their hearts and send them packing. This strategy had worked often enough with less determined groups, who had gone paddling back to their ships long before the performance was over. O'Hara was a different class of caller.

He had been chased out of Ireland for debt, forced out of England for being a Catholic, and successively hounded from Barbados and Jamaica for being a Royalist. O'Hara and the like-minded band he was leading were too desperate to be discouraged by a few missiles and an over-acted exhibition of black magic. They advanced upon the Caribs, who promptly withdrew in astonishment. Too much pork and massage had taken their toll. The natives had become soft. They mounted a fresh attack but their hearts simply were not in it, and they were so well camouflaged that O'Hara and party actually under-estimated their strength; otherwise the Europeans might not have been quite so courageous. A parley was arranged and a truce declared, leading eventually to a lasting peace with everybody's interests respected – well, almost.

O'Hara was an able and energetic man, – a farmer by occupation. Father Ignatius Kennedy, spiritual adviser to the group, was an enterprising Jesuit with a genius for organization. They had come prepared with sugar, potato, tobacco, hemp and other seed crops. Not everything they planted proved suitable or as useful as they had hoped, but they quickly transformed the internal economy of the

island. The Caribs were not natural farmers but their
womenfolk were soon conditioned to adding field work to
their other duties.

The settlers renamed the island King Charles, in
memory of their recently beheaded monarch, and as a
snub to Oliver Cromwell. They made their first settlement where they had landed – at the bottom right-hand
corner of the island – and called it Rupertstown to
welcome the king's nephew who led an anti-Cromwellian
expedition to the West Indies in the same year. Unfortunately Rupert failed to locate Barbados – though in
all conscience it was big enough – and his small fleet was
dispersed by a hurricane before it reached King Charles.
The compliment was not altogether wasted, however.
After the restoration of the monarchy in 1660 the island
was formally recognized as a Crown Colony with Michael
O'Hara as its Governor. Soon after, Prince Rupert
became a person of great influence in the Board of Trade.
It was thanks to his intervention that the Royalist
inhabitants of KCI were excused all export taxes for ten
years.

With the increase in piracy masquerading as priva-
teering against the King's enemies, Rupertstown with its
natural harbour came to enjoy great popularity as a
supply post during the last part of the seventeenth and the
beginning of the eighteenth centuries. Henry Morgan and
later Edward Teach – better known as Blackbeard – were
only the most famous of a long line of valued customers.

Parts of the island coastline on the north were also
ideally suited for the arrangement of wreckings – employ-
ment that the Irish settlers supervised with pretended
diffidence but which the Caribs took to like professionals.
The salvaged cargoes consisted mainly of slaves. O'Hara
had wisely decreed that the slave population should never
be allowed to exceed the combined number of settlers and
Caribs. Although his ruling stemmed from political and
economic rather than from moral motives, its observation
was to have profound and far-reaching effects, while

making him immensely rich in the short term. The
rescued slaves were sold on to Virginia. Ten per cent of the
price fetched was paid as a levy to the Governor, while
from around 1666 the slaves were carried in O'Hara ships.

It should not be construed from all this that Michael
O'Hara was primarily a selfish and greedy man, for above
all else he was a cunning one. From the very beginning,
King Charles was organized on apparently enlightened
principles. The first island constitution awarded each
settler family one hundred acres, and every mature Carib
male ten acres. The land allocated to the Europeans
tended to be on the flatter areas of the island – to the west,
the south and the east. Carib territory happened to fall in
the hilly north, around Mount Manitou.

There remained some 10,000 unallocated acres – about
half the island – which the Governor kept in trust for the
King at a peppercorn rent. Since very few of the Europeans actually wanted to farm – they were mostly sea-
faring people – and almost all the Caribs at first despised
agrarian pursuits as unexciting – it had been left to
O'Hara and Father Kennedy to manage the plantations,
renting back a good deal of the land, working it with a
small but cared-for slave force mostly owned by the
Governor and the Church. O'Hara's and everybody else's
sugar, tobacco and other crops were processed through
efficient, big refineries and factories on a 'co-operative'
basis. These were also owned by O'Hara.

Prince James River – there was no end to the sycophan-
tic nomenclature – naturally became Crown property. Its
sources lay in the wooded hills around Mount Manitou,
and while its course was plagued by frequent rapids and
in one place a gigantic waterfall, it did provide a rudimentary method of transporting produce by raft through
the long centre of the island down to the estuary in
Rupertstown. Logs for building ships and houses came
that way – felled from the wide strip of land that flanked
the river banks and which formed part of the Governor's
title.

It is questionable that O'Hara would have succeeded in creating what amounted to a personal kingdom had it not been for the blessing and complicity of the One True Church. The original settlers were all devout Catholics mindful of past persecution – grateful for deliverance and freedom. As for the Caribs, they quickly recognized the doctrine of transubstantiation as entirely consistent with refined voodoo and came joyfully to Mass.

Michael O'Hara died in 1713 at the age of ninety-one. He had long since been succeeded as Governor by his son John (1661-1742), the progeny of his formal union with a Carib girl following the death of his first wife in 1659. While the marriage cemented relations between the whites and the Caribs, it was also the reason why Michael had not retired to Ireland or England. Thus, in several ways, he set a pattern for succeeding generations of O'Haras, all of whom regarded KCI as 'home', none of whom married pure white women, few of whom failed to live to great ages, and all of whom – with the exception of the present generation – succeeded in producing legitimate male heirs, including Matthew O'Hara (1788-1869), who accomplished that ambition at the age of 72.

Nine generations of O'Haras have prospered on King Charles. Seven produced Governors – Matthew, the last of these, resigned the office on his seventy-fifth birthday in 1863 having first built himself an elaborate Gothic palace on the hill behind Government House: it completely dominates the other building. Both houses look down on the harbour nearby, and to the west.

For more than three hundred years the economic, ethnic, and religious order that Michael O'Hara set up on the island has underpinned a relative prosperity for the inhabitants – this in sharp contrast to the misfortunes suffered by communities in other parts of the Caribbean. The decline of the sugar, coffee, cotton and tobacco industries in the area did not bring disaster; KCI was not reliant on any of these except for its own needs. The failure of other island governments to produce sufficient fresh vegetables, dairy produce and meat only demonstrated their indifference to good example. The potato was only the first root crop brought to King Charles. Successive O'Haras introduced others, plus tomatoes, cabbages, and a variety of green vegetables, all farmed on an adequate scale. It was Matthew's son, Terence (1860-1935), who at the turn of the present century developed a cross breed of cattle ideally suited to the climate and feedstuffs available: these beasts tended to resemble undersized Indian Zebu but they milked like Jerseys and tasted like tough Aberdeen Angus.

The end of slavery in 1834 had caused few problems on King Charles. The newly emancipated actually made up a minority of the population, and virtually all were at least third or fourth generation Carleons – as the inhabitants of the island liked to be called; a title derived from the Spanish 'Carlos' was deemed preferable to being known as Charlies all even those years ago. Matthew O'Hara, schooled in England, had long been convinced of the inevitability of abolition. The education he afforded his slaves and the fairly generous land grants he made to them – mortgaged by their labour – ensured they were quickly assimilated into the free population.

By the end of the nineteenth century the population of KCI had become as close knit and isolationist as it is today. Nor had it been necessary to import Chinese and Asians to add to the ethnic mix when the need for cheap labour produced this recourse in other parts of the Caribbean. Sugar was the only – and seasonally – labour-intensive industry, and it was a relatively small one. The O'Haras as paymasters to the island balanced the agricultural output as well as the books. There was never any stigma attached to cutting cane because no one needed to rely on that temporary occupation alone for a living. Even in modern times the KCI sugar crop on the O'Hara estates is largely managed by hand and not machine, with no shortage of hands for the task.

Just as the founders of modern King Charles had been

seafarers, so has the tradition been carried on. Under sail and steam Carleons established a reputation as seamen and any excess of population has always been easily accommodated at sea. Over a third of the male population at any time in the last hundred years has been gainfully employed afloat – serving under the flags of many nations and remitting valuable foreign currency back to the island.

It is only fair to add that for the first half of the twentieth century KCI's healthy economy was in very large measure supported by an export the population had done nothing to develop and, albeit inadvertently, a good deal to hinder before its potential was realized. The younger Columbus had noted the incidence of bird life. Without question he was recording his observations of Gull Rock – a two-mile long and (once elevated) narrow island lying a short distance from the mainland, beginning half-way up the west coast of King Charles and skirting it northwards. The property of the O'Haras, the bird sanctuary contained one of the richest and most conveniently exploitable deposits of guano in the world. It took fifty years to use up this fortune – the single greatest source of wealth the O'Haras ever enjoyed.

The exhaustion of KCI guano available for export to the fertilizer manufacturers of the USA, and thus the reduction of Gull Rock from a towering outcrop to a small plateau a few feet above sea level, might have been expected to alter the island's economy as much as its western landscape. Happily there was no discernible drop in standards, nor in the ability or willingness of the O'Haras to ensure popular contentment through the taxes the family paid and the gifts it made.

The Michael O'Hara Primary Schools – there were five – the Ignatius Kennedy Memorial Grammar School, and the King Charles Agricultural College provided an adequate educational facility for the young of KCI. There were also numerous O'Hara Bursaries to enable promising pupils to continue their studies in Britain and elsewhere.

Various O'Hara Trusts had been formed over the years to fund the provision and future survival of a small hospital and libraries, as well as pensions for that very large percentage of the island's 7800 inhabitants directly employed by O'Hara companies.

The Roman Catholic Church continued as a major beneficiary of the family largesse – and the second biggest influence in the community. Other denominations were tolerated, but while there were Anglican and Baptist churches on the island, they numbered between them scarcely five hundred adherents, mostly lapsed.

There were no political parties on KCI. The Governor, appointed from the UK, chaired an Executive Council of three – the other two members were drawn from an elected Legislative Assembly of seven. This arrangement had obtained since 1882. Significantly, no O'Hara had been formally involved as a member of the Assembly or the Council since old Matthew had resigned the Governorship in 1863 and retired to his imperious new abode. Since that time successive Governors had been obliged to climb the hill to seek O'Hara approval or direction on any and every issue affecting the island's economy and organization. The Gothic pile had not been named Buckingham House without reason.

It was Patrick O'Hara (1890-1962) who had exploited the guano deposits and who, when these were exhausted, had thrown a good deal of energy into the production of King Charles Cigars. It was no surprise that after a fairly modest start this activity – in relative terms – grew to be immensely successful. After the Cuban revolution in 1959 the consumption of Havana cigars was declared an un-American activity, and it was natural that this created a marketing opportunity in the USA for cigars produced less than eighty miles from the Cuban shore. All this lent even greater credence to old Patrick's reputation for perspicacity. The fact remained that KCI cigars were in no way superior to Jamaican, and the output was small. Still, they fetched an enormous price on the American market as was demonstrated by the audited accounts of the O'Hara Tobacco Company, a wholly owned subsidiary of O'Hara Industries Ltd.

King Charles Island had not joined the ill-fated Caribbean Federation, so that it was hardly affected when that alliance disintegrated in 1962 – as Patrick O'Hara had prophesied it would. However, the last event was used to justify the holding of a referendum to give the people of KCI the opportunity of voting whether they wished to remain a Crown Colony or to become independent. Ninety-three per cent of the enfranchised population exercised their rights in the polling booths, and all but five elected to remain under the British yoke. The number should have been seven, but two of those instructed to vote this way – to offer proof of the absence of duress – lost heart at the last minute.

A visit four years later from the United Nations Decolonization Committee served only to confirm the astonishing fact that the islanders carried their colonial status with pride, and considered the whole enquiry to be at best facetious and at worst an affront to their individual and national liberties. The Committee members flew away bewildered – most of them back to homes in newly emerged countries torn by civil strife, political corruption and general famine. The inhabitants of King Charles, they ruminated, were a backward people quite undeserving of the contentment they enjoyed.

Joseph Michael O'Hara, the 63-year-old bachelor head of KCI's First Family, sat silent and thoughtful at his desk in the dark-oak panelled library of Buckingham House. He had always found the interior of his home conducive to contemplation. Being a man of some sensitivity he tried to avoid contemplating – or even gazing at – its hideous exterior.

The building in shape, if not quite in scale, closely resembled the Randolph Hotel, Oxford. As though the duplication of such neo-Gothic excess were not a sufficient shock to the unwary, the aesthetic strain was worsened by the emergence of an octagonal tower at the centre. This was a truly derivative feature, copied from drawings of Fonthill Abbey in Wiltshire, a folly that had the grace to fall down a decade after it had been built. Buckingham House had proved unshakably durable, arrogantly withstanding the ridicule and contempt of informed observers, as well as a minor earthquake in 1902.

O'Hara pushed aside the two slim reports he had been reading earlier and glared disdainfully at the instructions in the fresh blackmail note. This time the demand was for 25,000 US dollars – not a considerable sum in the circumstances – to be paid, as usual, into that numbered Swiss bank account. That would make $100,000 in twelve months – less modest when one thought of it in that way, but still a measure at once of the timidity as well as the cunning of his persecutor – something that further confirmed his growing suspicion of the man's identity.

Soon it was conceivable that in some parts of the world men would no longer be victimized in this way. Where there was general consent there could be no condemnation, certainly if care was taken not to involve minors. The WHO report of 1969 had been at worst ambivalent. O'Hara had never had a problem with his conscience – not a serious one. So why had he gone on paying? He paid because of the others involved; he did not consider he had it in hi soul to endanger others.

It was because of the blackmail he had decided to get shot of the whole business. He had always been vulnerable and for nearly two years he had paid to protect his vulnerability. The thing had become too big. Today it was one blackmailer; tomorrow it could be ten – and twenty the day after. No: he had made the right decision, in principle at least.

He had to admit he felt cleaner at the prospect – so

much so that he would ask Aloysius to hear his confession today, before their business meeting. That would be a surprise – it would also help to add credence to the minor deception he proposed. He regretted this last stratagem, but it was necessary. He wondered who heard Aloysius's own confession. From the first they had agreed that each must settle with his own conscience. In a sense it must have been easier for the priest – not because he was a priest but because he was a Carib, a true Carleon to whom the practice was in any case . . .

Joseph O'Hara shrugged his shoulders; it took all sorts. He glanced at his watch. He would need to hurry if he meant to be early for his date at the Presbytery.

The more pious of his friends and family were later to find comfort in the knowledge that Joe had received one sacrament so shortly before his tragic death.

CHAPTER III

'Well, you should have made it plain to Mr Gore and these Dogwall people that this is Government House, not an hotel.' Lady Rees gave another tug on her Live 'n Breathe All-in-One girdle and padded towards the full length mirror. She stared at herself accusingly. 'The Treasures are a different matter. My God, I'm a sight. She's quite famous. The guest-house is perfectly adequate for the others. You don't see Joe O'Hara volunteering to put anybody up. The people who make these things should be sued. Pour me another drink. Anyway, according to Debby, the Dogwalls are definitely NQOC.'

The need to take a breath did nothing to improve the credibility of the all-in-one promise. Constance Rees had a torso irreversibly divided into three bulges; litigation would not have proved otherwise. Grateful for the temporary cessation of the high-pitched, staccato soliloquy, Sir Archibald Rees dutifully poured a whisky and soda, while wishing his wife would put on some proper clothes. There was no denying Constance was a big woman; in that skin-tight undergarment she looked obscene.

'It's just that the Treasures don't arrive until tomorrow, Constance. We could have . . .'

'Had the Dogwalls here for a night and turfed them out in the morning to make way for the carriage trade. Really, Archie, even Americans have feelings.' Lady Rees was not without compassion. 'Oh, to hell with it.' She started to strip: this was not a pretty sight. The Governor turned to the glass Venetian door that led from the first-floor bedroom on to the centre of the wide balcony outside.

Government House on King Charles Island is an attractive stone edifice commanding a fine view of Rupertstown from the east. Georgian-Colonial in style, it had been adapted from a design in *The Builder's Jewel*, a pattern book devised by Batty Langley and published in London around 1746. Two wooden houses had successively stood near the same site – one had been completely destroyed by an earthquake, the other partially by a whirlwind. Governor James O'Hara (1726-1801) had been seriously inconvenienced and mildly embarrassed by the second of these disasters. He had been entertaining two Carib girls in his bedroom when the front wall blew away advertising his predicament to a large group of islanders sheltering in the church porch opposite. He emerged unscathed but determined to rebuild from a more durable material than timber – and further up the hill.

James had sent to England for an architect, but since none could be persuaded to make the journey he managed with the pattern book. The result, completed in 1781, was a sturdy building with seven window bays front and back, five to the sides. Two storeys high, plus a basement, the front was enhanced by the superimposition of covered colonnades on both levels, prettily balustraded and punctuated by eight pairs of slim Ionic columns, the centre four of these rising to support a pediment pierced by an oval window. The colonnades provided at ground level an elegant reception area and on the first floor a covered deck – or Captain's walk, a feature so beloved of architects of the period in the southern states of America.

Although parts of the attic space had been ingeniously adapted in more recent times to provide extra accommodation, the house was not large. Its rooms were big but few in number. Shortly before Governor Rees arrived, his predecessor had built a guest bungalow some hundred yards below and to the south of the main house, where the garden joined the beach. This was a long building which divided into two suites if required. Discounting any consideration of prestige, it was likely that the Dogwalls and Peregrine Gore would be a good deal more comfortable in their modern beach-side accommodation than the Treasures would be at Government House with its antique plumbing.

The early evening view of the town and harbour below was too familiar to enthral Archie Rees. 'And don't walk away.' Constance was emerging from the clothes closet with an armful of generously draped, voluminous long dresses; she had accepted defeat – the new, sea island cotton sheath dress laid out on the bed earlier could be flown back to Montego Bay next day. 'What am I supposed to say to these Dogwall people? Thank you for coming, but we don't think we'll be needing your ghastly hotels and nasty package tourists?'

Archie Rees had been thinking about a railway ticket. He was not planning a journey; he collected railway tickets. He looked back at his wife who was clambering into a black chiffon tent. Things might have been different. They could have been preparing for dinner in some European Embassy. In that event she would surely not have let herself go in the way she had. He would have been presentable in tails – or at least a dinner-jacket – instead of the worn white linen suit that passed for formal evening wear in this out-of-the-way place.

It was not as though he had started in the Colonial Service. He had been a grade one recruit in the Diplomatic in the days when the two were separate. 'Failed to live up to early promise. Unsuitable for higher responsibility' – that's what had been written on his dossier; he had seen it one day, by chance, carelessly and heartlessly left lying open on a secretary's desk in London. In a sense, though, amalgamation of the Diplomatic with the Colonial had saved him from further indignity. They had at least thought him good enough to run King Charles. That had been nine years ago. At fifty-six he was still lean – his tall, slightly stooping figure and scholarly appearance helped him look the part he had been sent to play. He had been given his knighthood – Buggins's turn, but it had pleased Constance. For his own part he remained bitter and unfulfilled. It was small consolation that in the whole of Her Majesty's Foreign Service there was no one with a more exhaustive knowledge of the long defunct Great Western Railway.

'The Dogwalls?' He tried to concentrate on his wife's question. 'Yes, well, we need to be civil to them in case Joe turns down the distillery offer.' He frowned. 'Though why one man should have the absolute power to . . .'

'Well, heaven alone knows why anyone wants another distillery in the Caribbean.'

Rees had already explained the terrestrial enough reason to his wife; perhaps he had gone too quickly. 'Joe feels the island is becoming too dependent on cigars. He used an international broker to offer . . . oh, very discreetly . . . the tobacco company to a few possible buyers at a very attractive price – I think one year's profits . . .'

'Yes, well, I don't see how that helps the island. Of course it lines Joe's pockets as usual.' Constance was applying liberal quantities of Cutex Flame Red to her fingernails, a process that appeared slightly to increase her powers of concentration.

'As well as being offered the tobacco company at a knock-down price,' the Governor continued stoically, 'prospective buyers were made to promise additional capital investment in KCI – in new industry here, as a kind of make-weight. In fact, it's an extremely astute idea on Joe's part.'

'I don't follow. They should thin out this stuff.' Lady Rees was vigorously waving one hand in the air as though desperately hailing a taxi.

The Governor sighed. 'I am trying to explain, my dear.' He wondered if it was worth it; he wondered whether anything was worth it any more. 'An Anglo-Australian group has offered to put in a distillery.' He went on more out of a sense of duty than in hope of spreading true enlightenment. 'They're represented by this chap Treasure – oh, and Gore who's dining tonight. World consumption of rum is on the increase.' He gave a guilty glance at the glass of whisky in his hand. 'The way things are going in Jamaica, the rum there may well become too expensive for world markets. A distillery here could be quite profitable long-term.'

'But the Dogwalls have nothing to do with the rum business. And he's not a banker – you said . . .'

The Governor had produced a folded sheet of notes from an inside pocket. He read from this. 'Glen Dogwall the Third – d'you suppose they have a kingdom somewhere?' He looked up, shook his head, then continued. 'Glen Dogwall the Third is President of the Sunfun Hotel Corporation of America. They're offering to develop the whole of the Rollover Bay area – hotels, villas, golf-courses, rafting – there's even been mention of a casino.'

'A gambling casino?' Constance was waving the other hand in the air as if in jubilation at the prospect. 'Surely Holy Joe would never agree?'   •

'One hopes not; one sincerely hopes not – but Joe has become so unpredictable. I mean, why has he suddenly decided there's no future in cigars?' The Governor shrugged his shoulders before inappropriately extracting a cigarette from a silver case. 'Anyway, he's down to a short list of two offers. Treasure is coming for more or less formal meetings. The Sunfun financial people are not due until next week . . .'

'So why are the Dogwalls . . . ?'

'The Dogwalls are taking a little holiday.' Rees cut in with uncharacteristic firmness, and as if to avoid further interrogation on the same line of enquiry he continued. 'By the way, Mrs Dogwall is wife number two.'

'Debby says she looks like a tart.' Debby was the Reeses' nineteen-year-old daughter. Educated in England, she was due to return there in the autumn to read history at Cambridge. 'Mr Gore, on the other hand, she describes as dishy.'

'Well, we can make our own judgements at dinner.' Archie Rees was not given to accepting other people's opinions. This and the fact that he rarely formed any of his own should have underwritten his success as a diplomat. What held him back was not a penchant for indecision but a penchant for advertising it. In the words of one Foreign Minister, 'Archie's problem is he's too bloody scrutable.'

Father Aloysius Babington was big, tall, black and very angry. He stood at the door of his Presbytery near the quayside regarding with disfavour the retreating figure of his most affluent parishioner. Joe O'Hara had left, as he had arrived, on foot. There was nothing especially symbolic about this. The climb to Buckingham House after passing the church and the Governor's residence was fairly steep, but Joe liked to walk, even though he owned most of the motor transport on the island. Already he was stopping to pass the time of day with people in the street – the people he was about to betray.

O'Hara and Babington had been close friends for more than twenty years; the priest was much the younger of the two but any gap in their relationship that might have been opened through age difference, or for that matter by status, riches or skin colour had been bridged by their common and almost fanatical devotion to the community both felt they lived to serve. It was no overstatement to say that they had conspired together – and at some risk to themselves – to ensure the well-being of all Carleons; their mutual trust and understanding would in all circumstances have been judged complete. Yet now Babington wondered whether he knew Joe at all.

The priest had long since accepted O'Hara's decision in the matter of the cigar company. In this he had been deferring to the older man's judgement – no more than that, for until an hour before there had been no reason to assume it had been prompted by anything more urgent than simple prudence. In the confessional Joe had announced he considered himself a thief – stealing money pledged to improve life for the people of KCI and using it to pay a blackmailer. The reasoning was, of course, ridiculous; it was Joe's money in the first place – simply money he had pledged to give away to the community: it was typical of the man to think of it as money morally beyond his entitlement.

It had disturbed but not incensed Babington that Joe had never before even hinted that he was being blackmailed – and that he had not sought counsel from his friend, even when he believed he had guessed at the identity of the blackmailer. The priest's anger and feeling of alienation had stemmed from a different source.

It had been later, in the Presbytery, that Joe had revealed his plan to accept the offer which would convert the west side of the island into a cheap tourists' paradise. Babington had scarcely been able to credit that the man he had trusted and respected above all others had been able even to contemplate such an ignoble course.

In the light of what he had learned in the confessional Babington was ready to agree that the days of the cigar operation were numbered. If the decision had been his to make he might still have applied himself to finding a compromise solution, given that it was possible to deal with the blackmailer. But the decision was not his, and he now accepted that Joe had serious grounds for what before had seemed an ill-considered action.

Of the two propositions that Joe had appeared to

entertain to provide income for the island when the inflated cigar profits evaporated, Babington had earlier supposed his friend intended to give serious consideration only to the distillery project. He had been flattered that O'Hara had sought his opinion on various propositions over the previous months. Only a few weeks before the older man had confided in him the intention to proceed with the distillery offer. Indeed Babington had regretted he had been indiscreet in quite inadvertently revealing his knowledge of this intention to the Chief Minister of the island before he appreciated that such an august person was not already also party to the decision. On that occasion he had been swift to acknowledge his error and to report it to O'Hara who had been all forgiving. That Joe should have changed his mind was beyond belief. How could the man who had done so much to protect the island in the past now be ready to see it converted into a centre of despoiling tourism?

The influx of alien, insensitive sightseers, the erection of garish hotels, the flaunting of riches by overfed seekers after tax havens – in this lay the seed corn of social destruction. The same malaise had already reduced island populations in other parts of the Caribbean to the status of disaffected rabbles – unruly and unrulable. It invented a sense of underprivilege, promoted political awareness, and produced the sleazy sort of democracy that led to anarchy and ended in tyranny.

Babington had argued all this with Joe to no avail; incredibly, his friend had proved immovable in his resolve. It was not as though the priest was opposed to tyranny in principle. Heaven could witness he had supported O'Hara for long enough. It was a tyranny of the extreme left that he feared – and the emergence of politics in any recognizable form. There were no politicians on KCI, and there never had been. He believed with fervour that politicians represented a parasitical growth upon society – a growth that unaffected communities should resist at all costs.

The Carleons had God, their own labours, and the generosity of a benevolent despot to thank for their present contentment. Father Babington decided he would do anything – yes, anything – to prevent the disruption of that satisfactory condition.

CHAPTER IV

The pretty Carib maid in the tight-fitting blue linen uniform rolled her big dark eyes. 'You wan' any help in da bath, washin' yo' back, dat kind o' ting, jus' ring de bell. Das de biggest bed on de island.' She gave a short giggle. 'I'm in a room at de side, and me name's Sarah.' She made a little curtsy and left.

Peregrine Gore decided he was going to like King Charles Island. He was also ready for a bath. On second thoughts he decided to take a swim first and debate the propriety of having his back washed later. The flight from Montego Bay in Jamaica had been bumpy and sticky. The airstrip north-east of Rupertstown was clearly capable of taking aircraft larger than the eight seater Brittan Norman Islander in which he had travelled. A private Lear Jet had been fuelling near the single hangar. Peregrine was not used to small planes, and the pilot had unnerved him by asking him to make sure the door was shut just before take-off.

The only other passenger had plied him with so many questions during the journey that Peregrine had emerged physically and mentally exhausted. This was an uncommon condition in one respect, his body being a durable instrument.

His interlocutor had been an agitated wiry Scot. Although Peregrine judged the man to be in his mid-thirties, early baldness, a permanently furrowed brow, and owlish, gold rimmed spectacles all served to make him look older at first sight – and a mite donnish. He had moved to the seat next to Peregrine shortly after take-off. Before beginning his inquisition he had pressed evidence of his identity upon the embryonic banker in the shape of a not very clean visiting card. This he had snatched back some seconds later without explanation but with a look that signified he considered the retrieval to be accepted practice. For some reason he had then myopically studied the card himself before replacing it with some care in what was evidently its customary position in a wallet crammed with frayed and yellowing papers.

Peregrine had noted the legend 'Angus McLush – Author and Journalist' before he was denied lasting proof of this admission.

McLush had then succeeded in extracting enough information from the incautious Peregrine about himself and his business to fill several newspaper articles, without giving his subject the opportunity to question or consider his motive for doing so. Apart from his name and occupation the only other information vouchsafed by McLush was contained in his parting remark in the tiny KCI Customs Shed. 'See you at dinner, I expect,' he had observed conspiratorily as he had whisked himself and a battered suitcase past the sole and uninterested duty official.

It was shortly afterwards that Peregrine had been descended upon by the big, hearty, blonde-haired girl – an event that entirely put McLush out of mind. 'Wotcha,' she had opened, striding towards him with a gait and manner that put him in mind of Aldershot and a poem by John Betjeman. 'I'm Deborah Rees – call me Debby – Governor's daughter, sent to meet you and all that. You'll be Peregrine Gore – any relation to Pamela Gore-Blimpton?'

Peregrine had time only to shake his head in denial; this seemed to be his day for one-sided conversations.

'Well, that's a good start. We were at school together – couldn't stand the little tick. Here, let me have that bag.' Debby had then taken a deep breath and hollered 'Amos!'

– a summons that prompted the emergence of a lean and
aged black retainer from the rear of an equally decrepit
and also black Rolls-Royce limousine.

Debby had swung the suitcase at Amos who had
caught it underneath with both arms and struggled off,
sagging, towards the car.

'He's our butler, first-rate chap.' Peregrine just hoped
the valued paragon would survive the following few
seconds. 'We're short-handed today. We've got a chauffeur but he's working on the puffing billy for tomorrow. I
see you had Angus for company – too weird – great buddy
of Daddy's, though. Knows about railways.' No doubt
there were other ways in which to win the Governor's
confidence.

Since car driving was evidently not numbered amongst
Amos's accomplishments it was the Governor's daughter
who had taken the wheel with Peregrine beside her,
feeling like a footman, while the exhausted butler recovered his breath in the capacious rear compartment of
the car.

The journey from the airport had been a short one but
by the end of it there was hardly an aspect of current and
pending events on KCI of which Peregrine had not been
at least partially apprised.

He was expected to dine at Government House in
three hours' time with, amongst others, Angus McLush,
Joe O'Hara, Father Babington, the Chief Minister and his
wife and a couple called Dogwall. Next day, being
January 30th, was a public holiday when the whole
island commemorated the execution of King Charles the
First with – inappropriately, it seemed to Peregrine – a
carnival. While he was obliged to share the guest house
with the Dogwalls he should feel no obligation to fraternize
since, in Debby's opinion, the couple were quite definitely
NQOC.

'NQ what?' Peregrine had seized the opportunity
to put a question while Debby, who had handled the big
car with ease on the deeply rutted road, had been obliged

to concentrate at a point where every semblance of a macadamized surface had been obliterated altogether for a distance of some fifty yards. The erratic and bumpy progress of the car seemed not to affect Amos who was soundly asleep.

'The rains did that three months ago,' the girl had offered knowingly, as though this explained instead of highlighted the inexcusable disrepair of KCI's presumably main thoroughfare. 'NQOC – not quite our class. You'll see what I mean when you meet them. Plenty of loot, of course. Turned up this morning in a damned great aeroplane – well, by our standards anyway.'

On arrival at the guest-house Peregrine had unloaded his luggage from the boot of the car before Amos was properly awake. Debby had explained the extent of the accommodation, remarking enthusiastically on the whole-some width of the double bed – a point that gave an enigmatic quality to her parting promise to come back later. Peregrine had considered her an admirable girl in every respect.

The large studio room and well-equipped bathroom that were the extent of Peregrine's quarters overlooked the beach on one side and a small swimming pool and patio on the other. He swam first in the sea and then padded back through the room to the pool.

'Hi there, welcome to King Chawlls.'

Peregrine gulped. The breathtakingly beautiful woman lying face down on the patio appeared at first sight to be unclothed. A second look established that while her back was totally bare, the most basic of the proprieties was covered lower down by a wisp of brown bikini that nearly matched the sun-tanned colour of the wearer's skin. The accent was American; the lisp endearing; the breathy delivery enchanting; the total effect devastating. She was long, slim and superbly proportioned. Her jet black hair she wore in a careless bouffant style that had taken hours of anything but careless professional attention to arrange. Big gold rings hung from her ears. Her gaze was steady

and frankly appraising. Her movements were positively
feline – and she was moving now, trying without success or
effort to bring together the unhooked ends of her bikini top
behind her back. 'Say, would you give a lady a hand? – I
guess I have this thwing twisted.'

Peregrine hurried around the pool. He knelt beside the
woman who was now supporting herself on one elbow,
one hand holding the ends of the bikini top. Her face was
turned to his. Their two heads were close. There was a
delicious scent about her. The eyes were still on his, the
wide lips parted in an inviting smile. Peregrine grasped
the two ends of the material and tugged them together.
There was the sound and feel of tearing. The garment –
what there was of it – fluttered to the ground. The woman
remained as she was. 'Gee, but you're an anxious one.'
The gaze remained rock steady.

'What's the praablem, honey?' The voice came from
behind – so did its owner, a towering man with the proportions of a well-preserved, middle-aged, heavyweight
boxer. He was dressed in a blue bush jacket, immaculate
white trousers and white buckskin shoes. He wore a leather
belt around the jacket, holstered and equipped with a
particularly lethal-looking hand gun.

'I say, I'm most awfully sorry,' Peregrine got to his
feet and held up the hook and eye as though he was about
to thread a needle. 'There's been a slight accident. I was
fiddling about with this lady's er . . . that is . . . er, I'm
afraid the wretched thing's come apart . . . most fearfully
careless of me.'

'You English?'

At least the chap was not intending to shoot first. The
woman was rocking with laughter while swathing herself
in a towel.

'I am, as a matter of fact. My name's Peregrine Gore.'
Tentatively he offered his hand to the man. It was
grasped immediately in a crushingly firm grip.

'Well, how dee do, Perry. I'm Glen Dogwall and this is
my wife Rachel – or have you two met already?'

'No, no,' Peregrine protested defensively. 'That is, Mrs Dogwall just asked me to help her with her . . . er . . .'

'I guess we're neighbours.' Mrs Dogwall was now standing beside her husband. There was obviously twenty years difference in their ages, but they made a handsome couple. 'Sweetie – ' she turned to her husband – 'do you have to wear that armowy all the time? I mean, it looks kinda unfwiendly – don't you think so, Pewegwine? Gee, that's a cute name.'

Dogwall patted the gun. 'Just so the word gets out, honey. We're pretty isolated down here – *and* there're no locks on the doors. When the help spread the word we're protected, that should keep things nice and quiet. Don't you agree, Perry?'

Peregrine was not even sure whether the possession of a firearm was permitted on KCI, but he had no intention of arguing the point with a man who already possessed one and who had come upon him inadvertently undressing his wife. The affair of the Field Marshal's mistress was still fresh in his mind.

'I gather the people here are pretty law-abiding, sir,' he offered, and then, remembering his research, he added, 'They get an occasional case of praedial larceny, but that's about it.'

'What kind of larceny was that?' asked Mrs Dogwall, arranging the drape of the towel so that one bare leg showed through provocatively.

'Praedial,' repeated Peregrine, who had never heard of it either until the week before. 'It means the stealing of growing crops – pinching bananas, don't you know. It used to be quite common in the West Indies.'

'Say, you're a mine of information, Perry. What business you in – you some kinda lawyer?' This was Dogwall.

'Banking actually – merchant banking.'

'Well, how about that. You with this Grenwood, Phipps outfit?' Peregrine nodded. 'But I thought a Mr Treasure . . .'

'Mark Treasure's my boss. He and his wife won't be here until tomorrow.'

'So, Perry, we're rivals for the King Charles concession.' Dogwall's tone and manner were both relaxed. 'Gee, I wish we could reach some kind of accommodation over this whole thing. My guess is there's room for everybody.' He turned to his wife. 'Honey, why don't you mix us up some of that rum punch and bring it out here. Perry and I could use a little talk, man to man.'

Half an hour later Peregrine Gore was back in his suite unpacking the remainder of his things, confident he had done an exemplary job worming the finer details of the American project out of Glen Dogwall. For his part, Dogwall was satisfied that Peregrine knew a great deal more than he was telling, and that the young man – obviously hand-picked for this assignment – was every bit as shrewd as his well-known, hot shot employer: either that or he was dimmer than a broken flashlight – but in the circumstances such a possibility was unthinkable. Peregrine had done it again.

Angus McLush gazed momentarily at the feebly revolving three-bladed ceiling fan above his desk. The effect of this instrument was almost entirely psychological; any violent disturbance of the air inside the tiny living-room would have led to a pointless redistribution of the dust that coated all available surfaces: it would also have further confused the untidily heaped and scattered typescripts, newspaper cuttings, photographs and letters that gave the room not so much a lived-in look as a wholly unkempt appearance. This description applied as well to the whole interior of the little cottage on the western outskirts of Rupertstown.

McLush was not a big-spending visitor who maintained a vacation home on KCI. As such, he would in any case have been unique since the breed was officially discouraged. In the event, formal restriction was unnecessary due to the total absence of accommodation suitable to the needs of the least discerning sun-seeker. Some visitors had observed that even the standards of comfort at the single hotel on the island – the Royal Crown in Rupertstown – seemed calculated to ensure an average stay of one night – as it happened, a perfectly correct conclusion.

The dilapidated bungalow that constituted McLush's sole abode anywhere in the world had been available for rent some years before when the King Charles Railway Company had felt obliged to provide its previous occupant – the senior engine-driver – with accommodation more suited to his station and not quite so close to his work. McLush enjoyed the noise of shunting wagons.

As a resident European freelance journalist, McLush was the convenient funnel of communication for KCI announcements to the world at large – not that there were many such. Indeed, it was more his ability to smooth or smother accounts of undesirable events than his professional capacity in any more positive context that endeared him to those who controlled the island and secured his status as a resident – despite a recently developed and inexplicable coolness towards him shown by Joe O'Hara. The small honorarium he was paid for his services was entirely commensurate with the less than onerous duties. The *King Charles Weekly Advertiser*, his nominal employer in this connection, required nothing more of him than an occasional article. Its regular staff was quite capable of handling unaided the ritual digest of births, deaths, marriages and other parochial titbits its owner considered adequate illumination for its undemanding readers.

If pressed, McLush would have described himself as an investigative journalist and author – but not so far as the affairs of KCI were concerned. He travelled a good deal in the Caribbean, and as a 'stringer' for a number of American and Caribbean newspapers was the unaccredited source of a very few not very illuminating stories or leads about public and private affairs in politics and business in the area. A safe base was an essential requirement for one engaged in such work. It was just such a base that KCI provided.

No amount of pressure would have prompted the Scottish expatriate to reveal the nature of his other and most remunerative source of regular income – more particularly since it involved an activity conducted from his servantless, bachelor abode without the knowledge of the King Charles authorities. Further, it was business fulfilled without the need to travel much beyond his own doorstep – and certainly not beyond the confines of the island itself.

Angus McLush was a secret agent. He could not have affirmed with any accuracy – even under torture – exactly who employed him to provide regular intelligence reports on KCI. He could say with reasonable certainty that the authority involved was non-Communist and, in the light of experience, unexacting about the quality of information for which it was ready to pay on a regular basis.

He had been recruited in the lobby of the Strand Palace Hotel while on a visit to London two years earlier. At the time the proposition had seemed as unlikely as the person who had put it – a small, dark man with a badly fitted wig, an artificial eye and a pronounced limp. McLush had concluded that any organization using such a conspicuous character for clandestine work was not to be taken seriously. He changed his opinion when he found a bank credit slip for three months' retainer in advance – as promised – awaiting him in his post when he returned to KCI. The bank was Swiss. It was always possible that the short, dark man had been disguised. This still left the matter of the false eye.

Normally, McLush posted his entirely undramatic monthly commentaries on the state of King Charles when he was visiting some other part of the Caribbean. This avoided the possibility of his dispatches ever being censored on the island, though their contents were so

innocuous as to be nearly suitable material for his occasional column in the *Weekly Advertiser*. Indeed, on one
occasion he had used the same copy for both purposes,
with only the most perfunctory of amendments aimed at
making the newspaper article the racier of the two.

He appreciated that he was very small beer indeed in
the Secret Service hierarchy of whatever nation it was
that retained him. Sometimes he found it difficult to
credit that his worthless reports were read at all. It seemed
more likely that they were sent for immediate filing from
the forwarding address in the Cayman Islands and in due
course shredded. He had certainly never assumed they
were examined on the Caymans. Since he was well paid
for his commission he had permanent misgivings on the
possibility of it being suddenly concluded after some cost-
cutting official sampled his submissions and justifiably
cancelled his retainer.

Thus it was that McLush spent less time than usual
staring at the fan – his regular source of inspiration –
before directing his fingers to tap out a report of some
consequence concerning his first-hand and exclusive
knowledge of the coming clash of commercial interests on
KCI. Here was an opportunity at last. A competent
journalist, he built a narrative on the information gleaned
from Peregrine Gore laced with political and ideological
innuendo. He acted quickly to match the 'URGENT
AND IMPORTANT' prefix he used to head the first
sheet – and also because the pilot of the Brittan Norman
had promised to deliver the letter for him that evening
when he flew on to his Cayman Island base.

What Angus McLush underestimated was the speed of
the reaction that followed his report – the entirely unexpected and incautious telephone call just before midnight, and the instruction which, if fulfilled, would
justify the payment for two years' accumulation of worthless submissions and the promised bonus of as much again.

CHAPTER V

Peregrine Gore had decided to take his bath without the assistance of the obliging Sarah. This did not prevent him from self-consciously experimenting to discover whether it was in fact possible to wash the whole of his back without help. He was somewhat disappointed to conclude that not only was it entirely possible but also that it would be a charlatan ruse to invite nubile female assistance to do it for him.

The bath faced the south wall and above it an antiquated but functioning air-conditioner wafted refrigerated breezes on to his half-submerged body; it also dripped a good deal of water in various directions while setting up a clamour that drowned the music on the portable radio he had playing beside the bath.

In the circumstances it was surprising he heard the voice calling to him from the other room.

'Oh Pewegwine, honey, are you in there?' It was Mrs Dogwall and she must have been right outside the bathroom door.

He switched off the radio. 'Er, yes . . . I'm, er . . . I'm in the bath . . . is there . . .'

'Well, don't get out on my account.' Was she too intending to volunteer as an ablutionary aide? If this was so much the custom on King Charles he would be happy to draw up a roster.

'Say, that's some bed you've got in here.' Peregrine was beginning to take a definite proprietorial pride in this temporary but noteworthy possession. There was a pause in the utterances from the other side of the door. Perhaps Mrs Dogwall was testing the springs. 'We're wight out of ice. Can we bowwow some fwom your fwidge? That girl's disappeared.' There was another pause. 'What's that wacket in there? — Sounds like you have a hundwed horse power faucets.'

'It's the air-conditioner,' he roared in response, heaving himself up with the intention of switching off the unfamiliar contraption. He grasped the centre control lever which declined to move up or down; he pulled it towards him. The already labouring motor made a valiant effort to rise to the extra call which was thus inadvertently placed upon its ten-year-old, unserviced mechanism. There was the sound of violent acceleration. The whole unit vibrated with such force and clamour as to convert it from an air-processing box into a self-propelled heavy moving object. Plaster was scattered in all directions as the pulsating box inched towards the baffled Peregrine, while issuing a gale of arctic air that pierced his unprotected flesh.

Close to panic, and unable to stay the progress of the mechanical ogre by frenzied manipulation of the various controls along its face, Peregrine at last located the electric plug above the machine that provided the source of its bounding energy. Standing astride the bath, he wrenched the plug from its socket – thus depriving the whole contrivance of its sole remaining contact with the wall. With a final judder, the oblong metal box tumbled squarely into Peregrine's waiting if unwelcome embrace. With an armful of air-conditioner, he balanced perilously over the water below.

'My, but that must be a twicky exercise. Is it good for the biceps or something?' Mrs Dogwall was standing in the open doorway. She was wearing her appraising look again, this time tinged with admiration, and what might have been frank speculation; Peregrine was in no position to gauge such niceties.

The victim twisted his trunk and with it the large emcumbrance towards his visitor. In this way decorum was partially preserved but on a strictly temporary basis. It was not so much a problem to support the machine, but every next move was impossible without assistance.

'Could you fetch Mr Dogwall? I mean I'm . . .'

'Why, he's in the tub, honey. Here, let me give you a

hand with that thing.' Mrs Dogwall advanced firmly
towards the bath, discarding en route a short diaphanous
beach jacket to reveal a white bikini of even more meagre
cut than the one she had been wearing earlier – though
this time she was at least clad in both pieces. Delicately
she stepped into the bath between the beleagured Peregrine and the wall. 'I'll take some of the weight while you
get a foot down.' She smiled up at him encouragingly.

What happened next was to be for ever etched in
Peregrine's memory. It compared in quality of horror to
the occasion when he had trodden on the skirt of the Field
Marshal's mistress. Too quickly he dropped one foot into
the bath and stepped on the soap. The next moment he
was falling backwards into the water. Mrs Dogwall
screamed but heroically held on to her side of the air-
conditioner. Inevitably she collapsed under its weight,
falling forward towards the totally submerged Peregrine.
The air-conditioner, wires and plug trailing, bounced on
the edge of the bath and because of a protective thrust by
Mrs Dogwall toppled on to the floor with a tremendous
clatter.

Glen Dogwall the Third came bounding into the bathroom, hand gun at the ready; Sarah brought up the rear.

'What the hell's going on . . .' The beefy American
glanced around him in stark incomprehension. Peregrine
surfaced and immediately assumed he was about to get
himself shot.

Mrs Dogwall collapsed with uncontrollable laughter.
'Come on in, honey, the water's fine. Say, do we have any
use for a wet air-conditioner?'

Shaking with mirth, she stepped out of the tub. Peregrine stayed where he was; there was not even a face
flannel within reach.

Dogwall put the gun into the big pocket of his bathrobe.
He smiled as though to signify that finding his wife in
bathtubs with comparative strangers was an everyday
occurrence. Shaking his head, he walked over to examine
the ragged hole in the wall. 'D'you get mad with it or

somethin', Perry?' He lifted the machine from where it
was resting at a drunken angle with disarming ease, and
closely examined the interior of the fifty-pound contrivance before placing it to one side on the floor.

'I say, I'm most awfully sorry . . .'

'Forget it, Pewegwine.' Mrs Dogwall had recovered her
composure. 'Next time I dwop by for ice cubes I'll
wemember not to dwess.'

The couple left, passing the giggling Sarah in the doorway. 'You wan' me to scrub yo' back now?'

Sister Helena made the last entry for the day in the
ledger, closed the book, and placed it in the desk drawer
which she then double locked. Tomorrow was a Holy
day and since the cigar factory did not function on
Saturdays and Sundays it would be unattended for the
next three days. It was for this reason that she would be
especially careful about making her final rounds.

The little convent – a group of unpretentious, whitewashed buildings – stands in its own two-hundred-acre,
fenced plantation three miles north-west of Rupertstown
and just below the northern foothills. Ill served by a
rutted, dirt road, the convent must be one of the few
religious communities that relies on a railway for efficient
surface communication.

To the east the convent grounds extend nearly to the
river that flows down the centre of the island before curling
to its estuary in the town's harbour. A mile to the west the
single-track railway line that follows the coast up from
Rupertstown here begins its inland curve towards the
hills and the base of Mount Manitou. It is at a point level
with the convent that a spur of the narrow-gauge track
branches off, exclusively to serve the little community –
just beyond the other and now hardly used branch line to
Gull Rock.

The track runs through the convent gate, and over the
short distance to the long building in which Sister Helena
was engaged. This is the factory where the nuns and

novices of the Order of Blessed Elizabeth the Apothecary
produce more than half a million King Charles Cigars
every year. That the gate, set between high wire fencing,
is normally locked is more a tribute to the self-sufficiency
of the Sisters than a mark of their disinclination to
encourage visitors – though it is that also.

The Order is small but industrious. Limited to the one
community on King Charles, its pious members are
drawn mainly from within the island. When not engaged
in prayer, some of those Sisters not domestically involved
are busily employed in agricultural pursuits around the
estate while others are permanently responsible for
making the cigars and for instructing novices in the same
art.

Some might well consider it self-indulgent and un-
worldly of the Order to exist in splendid isolation when its
members might more charitably be giving of their talents
to the community at large – in nursing, teaching and the
more customary employments of socially aware, educated
and avowed Christians. Such a view would, however, be
singularly inapposite, not to say unjust. The Sisters of
King Charles are not, as it happens, particularly well-
educated nor suited for training in the professions, yet it
has been through their conscientious and materially
unrewarded labours that the economy of the whole island
is so well balanced: for many years cigars have been to
KCI what whisky is to Scotland – if not more so.

In the context of world trade in cigars, of course, the
output of the nuns of KCI is minuscule. Even so, a
discerning and strictly limited clientele is more than
ready to purchase the output of the factory and to pay the
very high price charged for the product.

King Charles Cigars – known as Elegantes – are four
and a half inches in length, and torpedo-shaped; that is to
say, they are pointed and closed at both ends – a style
popular at the turn of the present century but now rarely
produced anywhere else in the world. But it is not the
rarity of shape alone that accounts for the popularity of

King Charles Elegantes with the five hundred American customers who every quarter received their ten boxes of twenty-five cigars, delivered direct to each personally by one of a small fleet of plain vans operating from the small Miami depot. All of these fortunate and wealthy few, mostly domiciled in the more exclusive parts of Florida, will attest the infinite superiority of the product over all other makes. Some ascribe this to the subtle difference of the King Charles leaf, others to the way the tobacco is cured, yet more to the special skill and devotion of the good Sisters. It should be added that the spirit of Christian charity is hardly reflected in the habits of the customers who scarcely ever share their good fortune with any but the most intimate of friends.

It has long been a source of solace to cigar manufacturers in a bigger way of business that the KCI production was strictly prescribed some years ago through an import agreement with the US Customs Authority. This set out the maximum number for annual importation at half a million cigars, at a time when demand was far below that total. Over the years, however, the delivery list has built up – always on personal recommendation – so that for some time demand has far exceeded permitted supply. Thus, the cigar traders at large in the USA breathe more easily, for, like the Customs officials at Miami, they can afford to regard the King Charles import with condescension and indulgence: it offers no real commercial threat and its contribution to US Government Revenue is insignificant.

Convenient as it is to have a King Charles cigar invested with the aura of a holy smoke, the part played by the nuns in the whole production process, while critical, has always been in a sense incidental. It is the King Charles Tobacco Company that has controlled the business and reaped the profits. In mitigation, the growing and curing of tobacco in large quantities, the purchase of packaging materials, the arrangements for shipment and distribution, the keeping of books, and the making of tax and excise returns is none of it suitable work for a small community of pious nuns. Naturally, the Order is modestly rewarded for its contribution, but the sum involved has been only a small proportion of the annual five-million-dollar revenue. Joe O'Hara, who owns the Tobacco Company, has always seen to it that the large income had been equitably distributed both directly as wages to his estate workers and indirectly to the benefit of the islanders in general.

The only piece of the Tobacco Company income not ploughed back into the KCI economy is the part paid over to Paul O'Hara – Joe's younger brother – who, living in Miami, looks after the delivery of the product. This last has been an uncomplicated operation not even involving accountancy, except for the settling of Excise duty. Customers are invoiced from the island and make their payments direct to Rupertstown. It should be added, nevertheless, that the younger O'Hara had for some time considered himself inadequately compensated for the part he had played – and that this had been only one of a number of contentious issues that had, over the years, led to the virtual estrangement of the two men. Their relationship, far from fraternal, had long since degenerated into a strictly commercial one, conducted at arm's length.

That so substantial a sum as five million should be generated by such a relatively small business is again a tribute to the excellence of the product, the loyalty of its customers, and their willingness to pay many times the price of ordinary cigars. Indeed, it is for this reason that the factory production has been strictly for US dollar-earning export. King Charles Elegantes are not available for purchase on the island – a source of some surprise and irritation to the few tourists who ever visit the place.

All hand-made cigars consist of a thick core of compressed tobacco leaf, a binder to hold this core together, and finally a wrapper leaf. In the case of King Charles Elegantes it is only the tobacco for the core that is grown on the island. The binder is made from imported, impermeable paper, and the dark Maduro wrapper leaf also comes from abroad.

The factory, a single-storied building with a low-pitched corrugated roof, is a hundred feet long and forty wide. The workroom runs the whole length of the building and occupies two-thirds of its width. The rest of the space consists of a series of unconnected storerooms solidly partitioned to a height of ten feet and thereafter steel-grated up to the open rafters – a feature that ensures the proper circulation of air and moisture throughout the whole humidified structure. There are no windows on the storeroom side of the building and those on the opposite side are barred as well as fixed and glazed. There are only two doors leading outside. One, at the corner nearest the gate, serves as an unloading bay for the railway trucks that bring dried leaf from the O'Hara Estates; the second, at the other end of the building, leads on to a little covered walk connecting with the main part of the convent. The loading door is secured from the inside when not in use not only by two padlocks but also by a steel gate. The door to the convent is also made of steel and secured by two deadlocks. It would not be an overstatement to say that the tobacco factory is the most impregnable building on King Charles Island. This might be considered yet another witness to the scarcity value of the product.

Sister Helena's desk commanded a view of the whole workroom from near the rear door. It was in her nature to move quickly – a habit that Reverend Mother had long regarded as inconsistent with the contemplative life. Sister Helena had thus developed a technique for making rapid progress without giving the appearance of doing so. By stooping and taking short paces she managed to maintain both speed and an air of sanctity. The trick was to keep her shoulders on a level plane. None of this fooled Reverend Mother, but it helped to placate her. In fact Sister Helena progressed from one place to another resembling nothing so much as an industrious ant. Although there was no one else now present in the factory to care if she picked up her long skirts and sprinted down its entire length, she did not alter her habitual staccato and outwardly decorous style of progress.

She tried the lock on the finished goods storeroom, then hurried over to the long wooden packaging tables. Here the cigars are individually encased in aluminium tubes to keep the aroma fresh before they are boxed, and the boxes sealed and labelled. Everything was in order. She then passed down between the two rows of tables where the actual manufacture of the cigars takes place.

All raw materials had been locked away as was the custom. She glided from one side of the room to the other checking humidity scales, rattling the handles of all the remaining storerooms save one. Having satisfied herself that the loading bay door was secure, she then moved back quickly to the door of the storeroom she had ignored on her outward progress, bending – but not stopping – to smell the tops of the tables outside and, with equal dexterity and economy of effort, finding the right key in her hand when she reached her objective. The tables had smelled of freshly applied carbolic soap.

Inside the room there was a perceptible odour but well within the accepted tolerance. Here was stored the extra ingredient that, laced down the centre of each cigar, provided King Charles Elegantes with their irresistible appeal. Stacked on one side of the room was a neat, high pile of plastic sacks sealed – not tied – at both ends: these were the 'crocus bags'. On the other side two hundred or so plastic trays with air-tight transparent covers were racked along the wall. The material in these was in a sense raw, but more often it is referred to as manicured: it looks like tea leaves, yellowish in colour.

Sister Helena jerked her head from side to side as she counted bags and trays. This duty finished, she moved to an extraction fan set half-way up the outside wall. It was drawing air from the room into a tall, wide metal flue, the outlet of which stood higher than the building, topped by an elbowed funnel so that its exudation joined the prevailing westerly wind – wafting towards the sea. The nun debated with herself for a split second before turning the fan control up a notch – electricity was expensive.

After a final glance about her, Sister Helena retreated to set the burglar alarm, to lock the outside door, and to repair to vespers, but not before she had secured the lock on the little room containing a considerable quantity – in weight and value – of high quality marijuana.

CHAPTER VI

'How do you do, Mr Gore.' The Governor was receiving his guests informally on the lower verandah. He had broken away from a small group of early arrivals to greet Peregrine. 'I hope you're quite comfortable – no problems?'

This hardly seemed an appropriate time to report a gaping great hole in the bathroom wall, the destruction of a whole air-conditioner, and the fact that he had twice compromised himself with his neighbour's wife. 'Oh, absolutely, sir . . . I mean, everything's going according to plan.' With luck he might yet avoid getting himself shot by Mr Dogwall.

'Daddy, you're not to monopolize Peregrine.' Debby Rees looked cool and wholesome in a cotton two-piece with a long skirt. Her midriff was bare below a knotted bodice. She took Peregrine's arm. 'C'mon, say I'm a sexy lady in this outfit.' She twirled herself around.

Peregrine checked that the ensemble was properly secured. 'Excuse us, sir,' he offered unnecessarily to the already retreating figure of the Governor. He looked at Debby. 'Oh yes, absolutely ripping . . .'

'Well, don't rip it yet. I'm not Mrs Dogwall.'

'Oh Lord, has that got out already?'

'That and your preference for mixed bathing. The worthy Sarah tells all – well, all she sees. Is there more?'

'No, there isn't – and I didn't ask Sarah to wash my

back.' He could at least protest innocence in one other possibly advertised connection.

'Silly; you should have. All the Carib girls do it – it's sort of traditional. You've probably offended her – and if you think she was offering her lovely young body into the bargain you'd be quite wrong. She's an especially pious Catholic.' Debby gave her companion's arm a vice-like squeeze which he found wholly agreeable. 'I'm Church of England.'

'But not beyond redemption.' They had been joined by Father Babington who had overheard the last remark. Debby introduced the two men.

A black clergyman was still sufficient of a novelty for Peregrine to make him study the face carefully: he saw wisdom and authority in it – if a touch of harshness in the eyes.

'I expect you're a Protestant too, Mr Gore?' The priest put the question in a near to patronizing tone. Peregrine nodded, though he had not given the delineation much thought since schooldays: in the Army church parade had seemed like an extension of the National Anthem. 'Well, don't let that stop you from coming to Mass in the morning.'

'Oh, we all muck in for that.' Debby's choice of phrase – though enthusiastically delivered – seemed inapposite even to Peregrine. The girl rolled her shoulders as if to excuse the obliquity – an action that for Peregrine produced a marvellously exercising effect on the cleavage beneath her already revealing bodice. Nor did the movement go entirely unappreciated by Father Babington. 'What I mean, Peregrine, is that it's the island's big day,' the girl continued earnestly. 'January Thirtieth is when they chopped off King Charles's head *and* the day the first O'Hara landed – over there.' She pointed in the direction of the harbour.

'There were three years between the events, actually – ' the priest took up the story – 'but the day is packed with significance for all the islanders. We have a Requiem

Mass for St Charles the Martyr – ' he gave extra emphasis to the full title – 'in the open at the foot of Mount Manitou . . .'

'And simply everybody goes.' This was Debby again. 'Seven o'clock in the morning, and it's a five-mile hike – unless you take the train.' The disdain redolent in the last phrase indicated to Peregrine that to retain his manhood in the eyes of this incomparable creature he would have to walk. 'Then we all raft down to Devil's Falls . . .'

'Well, not quite all – there aren't enough rafts. I'm Joseph O'Hara. Good evening, Debby, Aloysius, and our new friend is . . .?'

'Peregrine Gore the banker, Uncle Joe.' Debby let go Peregrine's arm to give the new arrival a warm embrace.

O'Hara was clearly past middle age but doing his best not to look it. Short and spare, he wore his curly white hair close cropped. The brown of the weatherbeaten face and hands denoted an outdoor life as well as mixed ancestry. The pale blue eyes were tranquil and kindly. The demeanour of the man was assured but far from overbearing. 'Then welcome, Mr Gore the banker.' There was no mockery in the tone.

'Hardly that, I'm afraid, sir,' said Peregrine with a modesty that was entirely justified. 'I'm to help Mark Treasure when he gets here tomorrow . . .'

'With our important deliberations. Has Father Babington been telling you there won't be much business done on this island on King Charles Day?' The nod O'Hara directed at the priest went unacknowledged.

'Only the half of it, so far, Uncle Joe.' Debby shifted her attention back to Peregrine. 'The Treaty Ceremony at the Falls is at nine, and after that there's no end of revelry for the rest of the day – and most of the night.'

'The carnival you may enjoy, Mr Gore, I'm not so sure about the boring re-enactment of my famous forebear coming to terms with the Chief of the Carib Indians.' O'Hara smiled softly. 'It has meaning for us older ones, of

course.' He glanced again at Babington. 'In recent years
I'm afraid the young have tended to reserve their energies
for the carnival here in the town. The Mass and the
Treaty Ceremony are not so well attended.'

'That's hardly accurate,' the priest said stonily. 'We
had over eight hundred communicants last year.'

O'Hara nodded. 'About one in ten of the population,
among whom I regret to say I was not numbered – I'm
getting too old for that early climb. I did walk to the Falls,
though and I shall do it again tomorrow.'

'Daddy can't understand why you don't take the train,
Uncle Joe.' Debby was evidently more tolerant at signs
of decadence in old O'Haras than she was in young Gores.

'Because, my dear Deborah, no O'Hara has ever taken
the train – or for that matter, any other conveyance – to
the Treaty Ceremony. I remember making the pilgrimage
with my grandfather in his seventieth year – and no doubt
I should have been obliged to do so five more times before
he died if I hadn't been in England. Thank you, Amos.'

The Governor's butler was sagging close by with a
silver tray laden with glasses of rum punch and other
drinks, giving the impression it would be an act of charity
rather than an alcoholic indulgence to relieve him of some
of the load.

All four members of the group helped themselves to
fresh drinks. 'Excuse us, Peregrine hasn't met Mummy
yet.' Debby took advantage of the break in conversation to
propel the young man in the direction of Lady Rees who
was addressing rather than conversing with a dark-skinned
couple. The pair were soberly and formally dressed –
almost too correctly in comparison with what the other
guests were wearing and for what had been advertised as
an informal dinner-party. 'Mummy, this is Peregrine
Gore the banker.'

Lady Rees, whom her daughter had interrupted, made
it plain she had been cut off in mid-profundity. She treated
Peregrine to an imperious but approving stare. Her
existing audience looked relieved. 'It's a great pleasure to

have you with us, Mr Gore. I'm afraid you'll find King Charles society unexciting after what you're used to.'

Peregrine hoped most warmly that this would prove to be the case for the remainder of his stay. 'Not at all, Lady Rees,' he offered with conviction.

'Oh, come, Mr Gore. When I was a debutante in . . . er . . . in London, dashing young bankers were in constant demand. I remember . . .'

'And this is Mongo Joyce, the Chief Minister, and Mrs Joyce.' Whether to make up for her mother's failure immediately to have introduced the others or simply to stem the tide of reminiscence, Debby once more broke in without ceremony or apology. This earned her a renewed glance of disapproval which she countered with a disarming smile.

Lady Rees recovered herself. 'I'm so sorry. The Honourable Mr Joyce is absolutely my husband's right hand.' The object of this flowery description, while obviously pleased at the application of his formal title, inwardly resented the implication that his executive function made him some kind of lackey to a constitutional Governor. He resented Lady Rees even more. Her failure to introduce him at the proper moment was typical of her conduct towards him: he cared less about his wife. He found the woman overbearing and condescending, and – the biggest resentment of all – in his own phraseology, she secretly scared the hell out of him.

'We're delighted to see you here, Mr Gore,' said the Chief Minister. He was a tall, good-looking man of predominantly Carib but some African ancestry; at thirty-four years of age he was the youngest head of government ever to hold office. He had graduated at the London School of Economics and been called to the English Bar before he was twenty-six. A protégé of Joe O'Hara's, he had latterly developed an assurance that predictably dimmed the sense of gratitude that had earlier coloured his attitude to his benefactor.

Despite his intellectual capacity and achievements,

Mongo Joyce could not rid himself of a quite illogical sense of inferiority nor the feeling that he had been beholden to others for long enough. There was a good deal of justification for both sentiments. By KCI standards his family had belonged to the under-privileged section of the community. In addition, as an intelligent social democrat he was more and more veering to the view that the distribution of power and ownership on KCI was inequitable – which it was, accepting that political and social evolution since the seventeenth century counted for anything.

It would be an overstatement, however, to say that Mongo Joyce sought a greater degree of power-sharing and control much below the rank of Chief Minister.

Mrs Joyce was easy to overlook – her husband was quite as culpable as Lady Rees in doing so frequently. Trim, if running to plumpness, she was not unattractive. Her demeanour was stoic rather than meek; it denoted tolerance, not resignation. Her marriage was sustained by the need for her ambitious husband formally to observe the more important tenets of the Catholic faith: she bore her private ignominy in the style traditional with Carib women. Teaching at the College and organizing tennis were substitute occupations; they did not compensate for the love she had lost and the children she had been denied. Mrs Joyce was a desperately unhappy woman, but nobody noticed and nobody cared.

'You climbing up to Mass with us in the morning, Peregrine?' Mongo Joyce rarely missed an opportunity to advertise both his energy and piety.

Peregrine nodded enthusiastically. 'And I'm coming to watch you make peace with Mr O'Hara, sir.'

'Call me Mongo, please – we don't stand on ceremony here.' Joyce had nevertheless been gratified by the spoken deference. He gave a loud chuckle. 'I'm not pure Carib, I'm afraid, but as Chief Minister it's traditional I go through the ritual act of surrender to the invading Irish on behalf of all the resident natives.' He glanced at Lady Rees. 'It's not so much a political ceremony, you understand, as folklore – otherwise I suppose I'd be bowing down to the Governor instead of Joe over there.'

'Is there any particular significance about your doing it all at Devil's Falls?' Peregrine was attempting to show intelligent interest.

'Oh enormous, my dear chap. We clasp hands at the very spot where Michael O'Hara and Chief Yago came to terms in 1652 – it's just above the Falls.' Joyce became more serious. 'Did you know we could have hydro-electric power on this island, Peregrine? Enough spare energy to cope with any number of distilleries . . .'

'Not to mention hotels, villas and other desirable developments, would you say, Mongo?' Glen Dogwall, immaculate and unarmed, had detached himself from the group close by engaged in conversation with the Governor. He was clearly on terms of some intimacy with Joyce.

'You've got a point, Glen. Power we could have – and any number of foreign speculators.' The Chief Minister finished with a grin.

Peregrine had not noticed the arrival of the Dogwalls. He had purposely avoided any further contact with them after his private demonstration in hydro-electrics. He had earlier left his part of the guest house quietly before walking up through the garden to the Governor's residence. Now that the couple were standing beside him it was difficult to overlook the presence of Mrs Dogwall. The long, black Grecian-style dress she was wearing had its simplicity considerably enlivened by the top to toe slits at the sides. The garment was as much a credit to the wearer's self-confidence as to its designer's ingenuity. It had a front and a back, joined at the neck but nowhere else. The contours of the apparently otherwise bare Mrs Dogwall were thus intriguingly revealed, most particularly in profile.

A silver rope loosely knotted at the lady's waist tantalizingly increased rather than reduced the startling effect and possibilities the dress created – it also provided Mrs Dogwall's sole protection against total exposure, at least at wind levels below the scale of light breezes.

Debby looked disconcerted; her mother appeared positively affronted. Mongo Joyce and Peregrine exchanged meaningful glances.

'That's a beautiful dress you're wearing, Mrs Dogwall.' The quiet Mrs Joyce broke the momentary silence.

'D'you like it? It's the coolest thing I have with me.'

'That's hardly the effect it's having on the rest of us.'

'By Jove no!' In thus enthusiastically supporting the Chief Minister's comment it seemed wholly unfair to Peregrine that the disapproving looks of both Rees women should be directed solely at him.

'I was saying to Mrs Dogwall earlier that it's really quite impossible to keep up with fashion in this place.' Lady Rees offered such obvious proof of her statement it was hardly necessary for her to have made it.

'I know, I hate feeling half dressed,' Debby added, looking steadily at Mrs Dogwall who was hardly dressed at all.

On the unspoken excuse that fashion was a topic for women, Glen Dogwall drew Joyce and Peregrine aside. 'Say, I've had a few words with Joe O'Hara. I hate to disappoint you, Perry, but it seems to me he's ready with the go-ahead for the Sunfun project – at least in principle.'

Joyce's first reaction to this statement was one of undisguised surprise – although it was difficult for Peregrine to judge whether it was the import of the message or the indiscreet way in which it had been delivered that elicited this effect.

'Mr O'Hara has neither been elected nor appointed to make decisions for us. The Council will approve or disapprove any proposals affecting the island's future.' The stony and formal admonition was in sharp contrast to the Chief Minister's earlier relaxed conversational style.

'Oh, don't get me wrong, Mongo. I'm not counting any chickens – it's just that the man said . . .'

Whatever it was that Dogwall meant to add was lost upon Peregrine who was caught up in the general movement towards the balustrade prompted by the activity in the bay. A substantial motor yacht had appeared around the headland to the left. It sailed directly in front of Government House, then, after passing the long stone breakwater, altered course to enter harbour. The young man turned to find Joe O'Hara at his elbow. 'What a simply beautiful craft, sir,' he exclaimed.

'Hm, beautiful but hardly simple. French built, a hundred and forty feet, triple-skin mahogany hull, two Napier-Deltic diesels, maximum speed thirty-five knots – and at one and a half million dollars the most expensive and unnecessary cargo coaster in the business.' O'Hara had recited the statistics with no enthusiasm and had finished with a snort. 'She belongs to my brother Paul,' he continued, 'who has evidently decided to honour us with an unexpected visit. I think I'll start my pilgrimage to the Falls after dinner and spend a peaceful night there in my cabin. Paul prefers – quite perversely – to sleep ashore when he's here, and my house, though commodious, Mr Gore, has somehow never seemed big enough to accommodate us both.'

Peregrine had felt flattered to be the recipient of such intimacies until he noticed they had been caught by at least three others in the immediate vicinity. It was at this same moment that Angus McLush appeared on the verandah. His apologetic expression as he made for the Governor indicated he was aware of being late. Since he was attired in the same scruffy clothes that he had been wearing on the aeroplane it was clear to at least two of those present that he had not been delayed through any involvement in the pursuit of elegance – or even cleanliness.

Peregrine and O'Hara noticed the journalist's arrival as they turned inwards from the balustrade. The older man's benign expression turned immediately into a dark scowl. 'If I'd known that blackguard was going to be here I'd have gone to the Falls *before* dinner.' O'Hara evidently regretted his outspokenness the moment after he had uttered. He looked up at Peregrine. 'Forgive me, Mr Gore, for that uncharitable remark. I am too much given to thinking aloud – a common characteristic in ageing bachelors, but no more excusable for that.'

CHAPTER VII

Debby strode across the track to the little steam-engine with all the assurance of a wheel-tapper. It was past eleven-thirty but there was much activity at the open-sided engine shed.

'Meet *Sir Dafydd.*'

In response to this injunction Peregrine looked about him in search of some eminent-seeming personage. Three greasy but cheerful mechanics smiled at him, but they none of them looked remotely distinguished.

'It's not a person, silly, it's an engine – this one. Didn't Daddy tell you about it at dinner?'

Indeed Daddy had done so. The only detail Peregrine had been unable to recall was the name of the 0-4-2 saddle tank engine built at the Hughes Locomotive and Tramway Engine Works, Loughborough, in 1878. A wood-burning brother to three 0-4-0 locomotives made in the same year for the Corris Railway in mid-Wales, *Sir Dafydd* had been rebuilt and the trailing wheels added in 1901. Its gleaming green and black paintwork and shining brass belied its century-old origins. Archie Rees had previewed that point – at length.

Peregrine had ample excuse for his single piece of forgetfulness. At the moment the Governor had been pronouncing the name *Sir Dafydd* – with a proper but disarming Welsh intonation – Mrs Dogwall had assaulted Peregrine's knee. His surprised reaction – a loud gasp – had brought a suspicious glance from Lady Rees. Mrs Dogwall had not even been turned in his direction at the time. She had been giving every appearance of hanging on the Governor's words while actually digging her long fingernails into Peregrine's anatomy.

It was this single experience that had enlivened an otherwise exceedingly dull and lengthy dinner. Every course seemed to have included bananas, and if this impression was not strictly accurate it was the somehow obscene appearance of that fruit in unexpectedly boiled form that had made Peregrine over-sensitive about the omnipresence of the West Indian staple from then onwards.

He had quite enjoyed the roast goat – up to the point where he had assumed it was mutton.

It had not bothered Peregrine that he had been seated, as it were, among the groundlings down the centre of the long table. O'Hara and Dogwall had been placed to the right and left of the hostess while Mrs Joyce and Mrs Dogwall had flanked the Governor. The Chief Minister had been even further below the salt than Peregrine and had presumably been expected to draw comfort from the place of honour afforded his wife – though this had provided little enough comfort to her. The lady had hardly uttered throughout the meal.

Bored with Mrs Joyce and intimidated by the alluring Mrs Dogwall, the Governor had taken refuge in a soliloquy about railways which had lasted through five courses. Since this was a subject on which he was singularly well informed and one on which all those within earshot were miserably ignorant, Sir Archibald had encountered no difficulty in stupefying his audience and enthralling himself. Mrs Dogwall had pretended attention but Peregrine was aware her interest had lain in another direction for at least part of the time.

The Governor's account of the battle of the railway gauges in Britain during the latter part of the nineteenth century had little bearing on his later description of how the narrow gauge came to KCI. The standard-gauge track that had long since prevailed in the UK was in turn a good deal broader than the two-foot-three-inch line installed on the island in the 1890's, primarily for the haulage of guano from Gull Rock to Rupertstown.

The survival and extension of the King Charles Railway had obviously been due to a disinclination on the part of those in authority later to go to the expense of building roads. Peregrine was appalled to learn that the stretch of road from the airport to the town was the best on the island. In the Governor's view, preserving the railway had been a stroke of genius. The rudimentary roadway that more or less skirted the island, he claimed, was very little used. Peregrine could imagine why. The railway, on the other hand, served the western flatlands for the haulage of tobacco, sugar cane, fruit and other crops down to Rupertstown.

It was clear that the transport of passengers had never been a priority with the Railway Company. Like the first Duke of Wellington, the O'Hara family had almost certainly taken the view that inland travel for common people would prove a source of social unrest. The railway was intended for goods in transit. If people had to be transported they were accommodated in open freight wagons temporarily converted for the purpose.

The Governor admitted to the existence of a State Coach, albeit also topless and reserved for the Queen's representative and his party – not exceeding eight – for special forays such as the one occurring on the morrow.

Like most railway enthusiasts, Archie Rees had been loath to admit that steam had long since been replaced by other sources of motive energy. He conceded in passing that the King Charles Railway normally relied on three Brush diesel locomotives of quite recent vintage to haul its trains. He even touched on their superior braking power over steam-engines when working in mountainous areas. Peregrine was later to recall this point in detail.

This diversion was, however, quickly concluded by the Governor reverting to the mainstream and climax of his discourse – a tribute to *Sir Dafydd*, the oldest narrow-gauge steam-engine in active use in the Caribbean.

Despite the assault on his knee and the speculation this produced, Peregrine had continued to pay attention while shifting his legs to the left away from Mrs Dogwall. Debby, who was sitting on his other side, returned the pressure thus inadvertently exerted on her own knee with healthy gusto, without interrupting the earnest conversation she was having with Father Babington opposite. Peregrine had hoped there was no one under the table taking notes.

Dinner concluded, O'Hara had made his excuses and left almost immediately. The others had lingered over coffee and liqueurs, and were still doing so at eleven when Debby and Peregrine had set off on a tour of Rupertstown. The suggestion had come from Debby, but Peregrine had readily agreed since he had been cornered by Lady Rees and was being closely questioned on the disposition of eminent persons and families with whom it turned out neither of them owned even a nodding acquaintance.

It was as though the carnival had already begun. Strings of coloured lights were laced around the harbour area and down the streets. Bunting of every description was hung or being hung from countless windows. In the main square, just a block inland from the long stone jetty that fronted the town, the finishing touches were being applied to a massive square platform festooned with flags, banners and yet more lights. There were people everywhere – not making merry, but sight-seeing like Debby and Peregrine, or else gainfully employed in the preparations for an event that would clearly involve the whole community a few hours hence.

Debby had insisted on a visit to the railway yard at the far end of the quay and just before the road and rail bridge that crossed the river mouth.

'She's all fixed to go, Miss Debby.' The slim, beaming African in the neat boiler suit and peaked cap emerged from the cramped cab of the little engine.

'Peregrine, this is Luke Murphy, our chauffeur and

the only man on the island except Daddy who knows how to make *Sir Dafydd* puff.'

Peregrine was getting used to associating Irish surnames with black faces. He smiled at the engineer. 'But how do you manage when you have to drive the car?'

'Oh, *Sir Dafydd* only comes out once a year.' It was Debby who answered the question. 'It's really on its last legs but you wouldn't get my father up to Mount Manitou behind a diesel – would you, Luke?'

'That's damned right, Miss Debby. He'll be on the footplate tomorrow, and that's for sure – goin' up and down like this.' Luke Murphy gave a loud laugh as he hung on to the sides of the little engine, bending and stretching his legs.

'At high speeds the thing behaves like a rocking-horse. Anyway, we'll be hiking, so you won't get train-sick, Peregrine.'

Peregrine was next shown the controls of the engine and pressed to demonstrate instant prowess and acuity by driving it solo for all of a hundred yards. Much to his own surprise, this exercise was completed entirely without incident.

It was later when the couple were leaving the yard that the accident happened. Debby caught her foot in a rut. She sat on the ground while they both examined a very hurt ankle. 'Damn thing's twisted, curse it,' the girl exclaimed – and so it was. The flesh around what had been – in Peregrine's view – a very shapely limb began to swell perceptibly. In a few seconds a lump the size of a golf-ball had made a dramatic and painful appearance.

'Can you stand on it?' He helped her to her feet.

'Just about – but I don't know about walking.' Debby staggered one pace. 'Ouch! – Oh, Peregrine, I shan't be able to do the mountain in the morning.'

The ascent to Mount Manitou seemed to Peregrine a less immediate consideration than the return to Government House. He looked about him. 'Shall we be able to get a car?'

'There's no proper road. I'll have to take the blasted train.' Clearly, they were talking at cross purposes.
'I mean to get home.'
'Oh, now? Not a chance. Can you ride a bike?'
It was some time since he had tried. 'Of course.'
'Then go back and ask Luke if we can borrow his – he's almost bound to have come down on it.'

A few minutes later Grenwood, Phipps's advance emissary to King Charles Island was wobbling along Rupertstown quayside on an ancient but sturdy bicycle bearing the Governor's daughter on the cross-bar – cheered on from time to time by loyal citizens who assumed the two were on a practice run and that the performance would be repeated in fancy dress the next day.

'I'd planned a swim down at your place,' whispered Debby with a pout. They were back at the house, standing at her bedroom door. Peregrine had carried her up the stairs.

'I still think we should send for a doctor.'
'Nonsense, I'm sure it's not bust. If I put cold compresses on it'll be bearable in the morning.' She paused. 'You any good with a compress? – There's a bathroom through here.'

'You bet.' Peregrine was also disappointed that the evening had promised to end so tamely.

'Then be a darling and go and soak a towel.' Her hands were already on his shoulders. She leant forward and kissed him gently on the lips.

'Good morning, Mr Gore.' Lady Rees was standing in the corridor resolute as the Rock of Gibraltar and dressed like the Widow Twanky. Her hair was covered in a turban and her face plastered in white cream. 'Forgive my appearance, we do not normally receive at this hour.'

'Oh absolutely. Er . . . slight accident I'm afraid. I was just going to help Debby with her . . . er . . . her foot.'

'Indeed, Mr Gore?' The tone implied more than plain disbelief at the suggestion that young men hung about bedroom doors after midnight to further the cause of pedicure.

Debby's giggled but explicit account of her adventure and the reason for Peregrine's presence served to mollify her mother. This nevertheless put an end to the aspirations Peregrine had been harbouring about ministering to needs existing and developing, anatomical or emotional, in what had lately been his patient. Quietly cursing the rutted roads of KCI, he made his way through the garden impervious to the noise of crickets, the stillness of the night, the exotic nature and scents of the vegetation, and the soft sound of the sea wash. It was all as romantic as Aldershot Barracks to one just deprived of a guard duty he would heartily have enjoyed.

He opened the door to his room. The place had been shuttered in his absence and the shaft of light from the door provided only the dimmest illumination.

'Gee, Pewegwine, I thought you'd never get here.' The languorous voice came from the bed, and the identity of the owner was unmistakable. 'Old Glen is living it up with the Chief Minister so I thought I'd dwop by for a swim.' Mrs Dogwall might have been off course for the pool but the direction of her thoughts seemed sure enough. 'You wanna get –' she sighed audibly – 'chwanged?'

Angus McLush was a careful man. In the event of discovery, the evidence he was now preserving and compiling would only serve as mitigation for his crime. As others had discovered in the past, the miscreant's plea that he was only obeying orders sounded hollow enough to all objective judges. Even so, the foreign power that employed McLush, whichever it might be, must have some status in the world – and if he had guessed its identity correctly, it had a great deal. This, in turn, meant that help could – even should – be provided if anything went wrong. One read of agents being disowned in such circumstances but he had always considered this an unlikely event – a misconception perpetuated by fiction-writers. The embarrassment of exposure was something that must surely weigh heavier with sovereign states than upon individuals. Without doubt 'blown agents' were extricated. He dismissed the purported notion that they were also sometimes eliminated: romantic fiction again.

He would have felt a good deal more secure in these conclusions if he had been certain that it was the CIA that retained him. Indeed, he was sober and sensible enough to appreciate that the 'embarrassing exposure' of a foreign power he could not identify hardly warranted the description. But tomorrow he intended to settle the matter once and for all. He was then to be contacted in person and he had already worked out a plan to ensure that the contact was obliged to name their joint employers before getting off the island again. KCI was home ground for McLush, and if 'they' were daft enough to let another of their operators into his territory, then they must be prepared for the consequences.

He had had the presence of mind to tape the midnight telephone conversation. Whatever the consequences of his mission, at least he could prove he had been acting under orders from 'them'. He placed the cassette in an envelope and sealed it. Next he took the package to the bathroom and taped it to the underside of the cover to the water-closet tank. This was an awkward operation since it involved standing on the seat to remove the cast-iron plate of the old-fashioned contrivance above. McLush had learned this ploy from watching a spy movie – so fiction had its uses.

After collecting the equipment he was taking with him, the journalist left through the rear door of the little house. This conscious act of circumspection was largely nullified in its effect because the door in question had to be slammed hard to make it close properly. Apart from signalling McLush's departure, the vibration thus set up severed the last vestige of contact between the adhesive tape and the tank cover in the bathroom. The envelope and its contents fell into the water, floated momentarily, and then quietly sank to the bottom.

CHAPTER VIII

It would not only be uncharitable but also inaccurate to conclude that the lessons of experience had been entirely lost upon Peregrine Gore. Taking the Field Marshal's mistress to his room – at her request – in order to carry out repairs to her skirt had been a mistake. In retrospect so much had been obvious: in fairness, Peregrine had not been aware of the lady's special status – he had taken her for an unattached guest at a regimental party – nor had he known of her appetite for young officers. All had been revealed when the Field Marshal himself had arrived and at the moment when his paramour was giving maximum meaning to the phrase.

The events and consequences of that episode had so imprinted themselves on Peregrine's mind that his retreating through the guest-house door faster than he had entered should be counted as nothing more than a reflex action on his part. The siren call of Mrs Dogwall, while compulsive in its own way, would be insignificant compared to the blast of her husband's six-shooter.

Though Peregrine felt no immediate sense of ignominy in so unceremonious a withdrawal, he soon became conscious of the inconvenience involved. It was now twelve-thirty and here he was cut off from possession of his rightful living quarters – and his frequently admired bed – by a predatory female who showed no signs of yielding except in all the wrong contexts. He lurked behind a tree in the garden for some minutes with an increasing feeling of deprivation. Mrs Dogwall did not emerge on the patio. The possibility that she might have returned to her own part of the guest-house through the door on the beach side of the building was one Peregrine was unprepared to test.

He toyed with and dismissed the notion of returning to

Government House. Sleeping where he was in the garden would pose no hardship except that he was not in the least sleepy. The awareness of this fact came as something of a surprise until he concluded that the half-hour nap he had taken before dinner had temporarily replaced a night's rest inside his jet-lagged metabolic cycle; in the England he had left only twenty hours earlier it was nearly getting-up time.

It was this realization that spurred him to the idea of climbing to Mount Manitou ahead of the morning crush. He was properly dressed for a church service since he was still wearing the lightweight suit he had put on for dinner; he had shaved just before his bathroom encounter with Mrs Dogwall and thus, to all outward appearances, would be reasonably presentable up to lunch-time. Debby had given him firm instructions about a route past Devil's Falls and on to the Mount. She had explained the walk would take an hour and he concluded it might be a lot more agreeable making such an expedition in the cool night than even in the earliest morning sunlight.

The notion of a nocturnal expedition in a strange land was wholly attractive to an ex-Guards officer quite used to such a test of initiative. It was thus with resolution that Peregrine set off firmly – in the wrong direction.

On an island only five miles wide it is, of course, virtually impossible truly to be lost for very long. If one happens to be traversing its seven-mile length the experience could, theoretically at least, be more prolonged, but not by much. Happily, Peregrine had no sooner passed the imposing rear gates of Buckingham House than he was spared the inconvenience of suffering either maxima.

'Mr Gore, isn't it?' The unexpected salutation took Peregrine completely by surprise. He recognized the voice and then the figure of O'Hara – though both had seemed to materialize out of thin air. 'Sorry if I startled you, but you did the same to me.' O'Hara emerged from the shadow of the gatepost into the moonlight. He was dressed like a scout-master complete with wide, flat

brimmed hat and a stout walking stick. The khaki shorts
were baggier and longer than those currently in vogue;
indeed, the whole ensemble gave the wearer a distinctly
pre-war appearance. Closer inspection proved the first
impression; KCI's top citizen really was in the uniform of
the Boy Scout movement, albeit in a version long out-
dated by the fashion prevailing elsewhere in the world.
Only the machete clasped awkwardly in his left hand
introduced an incongruous note. 'Bit elderly even for a
Chief Scout,' he volunteered in answer to Peregrine's
unspoken question. 'Took me years to settle on the right
rig for the Treaty Ceremony. My grandfather used to
dress up like a seventeenth-century sea captain; my father
liked to wear his Great War uniform.' O'Hara spread his
arms wide and surveyed what he could see of himself.
'Since I am the Chief Scout hereabouts I think this does
very well – not as silly as fancy dress and anything more
official gets up the nose of the Governor. Where you off
to?'

'Mount Manitou, sir. Thought I'd get there early,'
Peregrine explained lamely.

'Well, you're more likely to be late starting up that path.
They should have given you a guide. Anyway, I'll be
delighted to perform that function – and very glad of your
company. I intend spending what remains of the night at
our cabin near the Falls – you're welcome to do the same.
There's a path from there that'll get you to the Mass in
twenty minutes. Wouldn't care to carry this thing for me,
I suppose?' O'Hara indicated the machete. 'It's my prop
for the ceremony. I exchange it with the Chief Minister
for a spear. Very symbolic.'

Peregrine accepted the implement. 'Is that what your
ancestor did on the first occasion, sir?' He fell in beside
his new patron.

O'Hara seemed mildly surprised at the question. 'I've
really no idea. But it adds colour, wouldn't you think?' He
smiled. 'Couldn't you sleep?'

'Afraid not,' Peregrine answered with accuracy. Apart

from his feeling of wakefulness, he doubted the presence of Mrs Dogwall would have proved soporific.

'Nor me. I've just had the most glorious up-and-downer with my brother – happens every time we meet, which fortunately isn't very often. Paul likes the bright lights.'

'He doesn't live on the island?'

'Good Lord no. He lives off it though – at Miami Beach; perfectly horrible place. Watch your step here.' The dirt path they were following had been flanked by tall sugar canes along its six-foot width. The warning related to a small and rickety bridge that crossed a narrow irrigation canal. The route took them behind the town, and some minutes later a broad river appeared on the left. 'That's Prince James River; we'll be keeping to it a good deal of the way. D'you row?'

Peregrine wished someone would ask him about squash or rugby football; he played both. His practice as an oarsman was rustier than his experience on a bicycle. He feared O'Hara might be about to reveal the existence of a coxless pair in which they could continue their progress against the fast-flowing current. 'Actually, no. I've done a bit of canoeing.' Despite O'Hara's earlier insistence on the traditional necessity of walking to the Falls, making the journey in a dug-out might conceivably have been in more accurate emulation of his ancestor's method of progress in 1652.

'We don't do either here – current's too strong and there are too many rapids and shallows. Rafting's fun, though – coming down, at least. Used to be the way they brought things to market – there's still a bit of river traffic. Look, there's a raft moored on the other side.' He pointed to a narrow platform of bamboos some twenty feet long. 'They punt 'em from the front. With a seat on the back it's quite a joy-ride for passengers. In Jamaica it's a big tourist attraction. Here we'd have to break the journey at Devil's Falls.' O'Hara spoke more as though he were planning a project than simply making conversation. 'It's one of the things your friend Dogwall is quite keen about.'

'And you, sir? I mean, you don't have many tourists yet, do you?' Peregrine put the question in what he considered to be a disarmingly casual style.

'Your circumspection does you credit, Mr Gore.' The style was admired, but O'Hara was far from disarmed. 'If you mean do I enjoy the prospect of this beautiful island being overrun by tourists, my answer is frankly no. However, needs must: if the thing is properly controlled I think we could become a profitable paradise.' O'Hara gave a quick, bitter laugh before continuing. 'You see, we've always had a balanced economy here, and nowadays we're too dependent on cigars for a living. It can't last for ever.'

'You mean smoking may become illegal?'

O'Hara started at what should have been an innocuous if unlikely suggestion. Then, satisfied that Peregrine's question could be taken at its face value, he answered, 'I doubt that. I've never smoked myself, though; it's a dirty as well as an unhealthy habit.' Which seemed a suitable enough rejoinder from a scout-master.

'Was the economy any better balanced when the island depended on guano?'

'Not really; and you've got a point, of course. Cigars took over from bird-droppings as our staple export, and now I fear we may soon have to find something to replace cigars. Tourism could do it. Rum, I fear, won't – not unless the free-world production drops considerably, or the price rises – or both.'

'I thought King Charles Cigars were very much in demand, sir.'

'These fads are often short-lived. We've kept up demand by creating shortage. The product is not that remarkable' – nor was it, in its basic form. 'The production costs have become so great I'm seriously thinking of phasing the thing out entirely. The land where we grow the tobacco could be put to much better use . . .'

'Under sugar, sir?' Peregrine was doing his best to

represent the rum lobby.

O'Hara smiled. 'In certain circumstances, yes. Mr Dogwall has golf-courses and villas in mind.'

'Could I ask . . . I mean, if it isn't rude, sir . . . have you got Mark Treasure and Mr Dogwall here together on purpose?'

They had temporarily left the river bank and were following a path over rising ground. O'Hara stopped as though humouring a whim – a doctor might have divined a more serious reason for the halt. 'There's a fine view both ways from here in daylight – not bad now, come to that.' He paused. 'You could hardly credit coincidence – and neither will your Mr Treasure. If you want the truth, our well-intentioned but misguided Governor invited the Dogwalls, once your dates were fixed, in the conviction that I should find the Americans and their purposes so ignoble in the comparing that I would dismiss them. He was quite wrong, I'm afraid. Pity; it's the one attempt at subtle diplomacy he's ever engineered to my knowledge and it's backfired. Come, we'd better push on.'

Peregrine was finding his companion surprisingly expansive. 'You mean, you've gone off the distillery project, sir?' The possibility that he, 'advance-party Gore', might get the blame if this was so loomed large in his mind.

'Well, it's just not on, my boy, compared to the other idea. Tourism is labour-intensive, distilling rum isn't. And tourists will bring in enough foreign currency to make up for the loss on cigars.' Peregrine thought it best not to enquire any more about the imminent collapse or closure of the cigar trade. 'Even my brother has got his mind around that simple fact.'

'Is your brother against the distillery too, sir?'

'My brother's against anything that threatens his personal income from our companies. No, he's not against the distillery. He's more in favour of expanding the cigar business. Madness, madness.' O'Hara seemed with these last utterances to be ruminating to himself rather than addressing his companion.

'I suppose all the decision-making is up to you, sir?' Peregrine had tried to make the question sound complimentary.

O'Hara grinned. 'I doubt you'll find anyone to disagree about that – though it sticks in their throats – some of them. It's probably difficult for you to understand. Doesn't sound very democratic and so on. But you see, we O'Haras have looked after the people of this island for more than three hundred years – and nobody's ever starved here in all that time. God gave us a great trust and woe betide the O'Hara who forgets it.' The older man's face stiffened. 'And God help the man who thinks he's earned the right to challenge my judgement.' He looked keenly at Peregrine. 'You know what I mean by *noblesse oblige*?'

'I think so, sir.'

'It's a code you make a way of life if you're born into a position such as mine. You don't stint your effort, you dedicate yourself to the well-being of those in your charge, and above all you don't seek to improve your own lot at the expense of the common good.' O'Hara spoke quietly but with great conviction. Peregrine was impressed – but he was also somehow uneasy.

A history master at Wellington College who had despaired of this particular pupil might at that moment have drawn comfort from knowing his labours had not been entirely in vain. Somewhere in Peregrine's mind there lurked the residue of a tutored conviction. The doctrine of the Divine Right of Kings, he knew, had sometime taken a fearful beating – and justifiably so.

Father Babington rose from the anguish of his devotions. He was hardly conscious of time, only vaguely aware that he had been on his knees in the Presbytery for several hours and that in only a few more he must be the chief celebrant at the crowded service on the mountainside. But his thoughts were not of priestly office, only of his responsibilities as a leader, and a Carleon.

The agony of decision still lay heavily upon him, even though the decision had been made. In any other context he could have – would have – taken counsel from a superior in the church or, he ruminated bitterly, from Joe O'Hara himself.

Instinctively, from his youth up, Babington had subscribed to the conviction that Joe knew best. Not until the conversation after he had heard the older man's confession had he ever found compelling reason to question that conviction. His strongest sense was still one of betrayal.

He had argued with himself – God knew he had argued these several hours past – but there was no escaping that Joe was negating the very principles they had both so often pledged themselves to defend. The cost of that defence for the priest had sometimes been very high indeed. By putting his responsibility as a Carleon before all else, by seeking to protect the material as well as the spiritual well-being of his fellow islanders, by subverting the innocence of others under Christian vows he had created what had often been a torment of conscience for himself. The expiation had been in Joe's dedication and the example of Joe's selflessness. The satisfaction had been to watch a people live in harmony and dignity without loss of their independence to alien paymasters or cultures.

The priest was well enough aware that the independence on King Charles had always been in the gift of one man, but that man had exercised his power with charity and humility. Joe O'Hara had earned the respect he was just about to betray – something that made the act even more terrible: something that made it necessary for him to be stopped.

CHAPTER IX

Glen Dogwall gave a loud burp. The utterance seemed hardly to register with Mongo Joyce, now in shirt-sleeves and tieless. Judging by appearances neither man could have passed a sobriety test. Dogwall was leaving the Chief Minister's house; they had repaired there for a night-cap an hour before. Mrs Joyce had fetched the drinks and gone to bed, after saying good-night to her husband as well as their guest; Dogwall had noticed this.

'I'll walk you to the end of the road.'

'Oh, don't put yourself out, Mongo; you must be tired – I can find my way.' It was no great distance back to the grounds of Government House. The Chief Minister's unpretentious home was at the end of a cul-de-sac; there were five or six similar neat, modern houses in the short street, each with about half an acre of garden.

Joyce continued at the other's side, despite the well-mannered protestation. 'You've got it clear now, Glen? Joe O'Hara may own the land, but I'm telling you, man, nobody gets a hamburger concession on this island from now onwards without official approval: no way.'

'Mongo, I understand.' Dogwall sincerely wished he did but he was still as much in the dark about what motivated the Chief Minister's personal attitude as he had been at the start of the evening. Either the guy was playing it straight for democracy or he was looking for a pay-off.

Twice earlier Dogwall had missed the opportunity cautiously to introduce the prospect of a bribe – a sweetener to secure that high-toned 'official approval'. Each time he had hesitated. Joyce's advertised reputation was that he was incorruptible. Dogwall's background and experience led him to doubt this virtue – in Joyce or anybody else. If the Chief Minister did have a price, then relatively it could not be very high. Whatever Joyce might say, it was O'Hara who ran KCI – the so-called Government was so much dressage. Even so, the Sunfun Hotel Corporation of America never failed to take a Chief Minister on the team if one was available.

They stopped at the end of the road. 'Mongo, I guess O'Hara will be doing pretty well out of this deal – for himself, I mean. OK, so we both know he's Mr Big in these parts, and now he's made it pretty clear he's giving us the go-ahead I guess I was inclined to ignore the er . . . interests of the other er . . . powers in the land.'

A small spaniel dog completed the almost impossible feat of squeezing beneath the gate of the end house, shook itself, then bounded up to Joyce and began prancing around his feet. 'Sit, Zako.' The dog immediately obeyed with the look of wounded innocence common to its kind.

The episode hardly registered with Dogwall who was carefully watching the Chief Minister's face. He saw nothing in the expression that discouraged him from continuing. 'In your own case I know the expenses of office, of living – keeping up standards generally – gee, they must be horrendous these days.' Joyce gave a just perceptible nod – the speaker was sure it was a nod of encouragement. 'Mongo, old man, lemme come to the point – man to man; know what I mean?' The guy was still all attention; this was going to be a push-over after all. 'What I had in mind was fifty thousand dollars now and another fifty when the contract's – '

Dogwall, being a big man, went down heavily. The professional blow to the solar plexus was so effective that Joyce had no need to follow through with the planned uppercut to the jaw.

'Go home, Mr Dogwall. And I mean home.' The Chief Minister, trembling with fury, stood his ground. The astonished, winded American picked himself up, prepared to retaliate, thought better of it, gasped, and turned on his heels. He did not see Joyce pause to recover himself, then slowly walk up the drive of the house from where the dog appeared, the animal at his heels. Still less

could he read his assailant's thoughts and know that just
as a hundred thousand dollars was not nearly enough to
buy Mongo Joyce, so any chance of the Sunfun project
progressing further had just evaporated – no matter who
favoured it. The decision Joyce had made cut Joe O'Hara
right out of the picture.

'Magnificent, isn't it?' O'Hara shouted above the roar of
the waterfall.

'Terrific, sir.' Peregrine was genuinely impressed with
the two-hundred-foot cascade. They were standing below
the Falls on the eastern bank of the river.

O'Hara was glowing with lordly pride. 'There was
talk after the war of harnessing this for a hydro-electric
scheme. My father got Westinghouse to put up a plan but
he jibbed at the cost. Pity in a way. Of course we'd have
been overpowered for an island this size but with the cost
of oil these days it might have been a good investment.' He
gazed ruminatively at the torrent of water. 'Mongo Joyce
has been getting at me to reconsider the idea.' He shrugged
his shoulders. 'Well, come on, it's a bit of a pull to the
top.'

Five minutes later the two were standing on a wide
plateau of ground gained by following a steep and
circuitous path from the foot of the Falls. O'Hara was pale
and breathless. 'If we ever do go in for hydro-electrics the
first thing we'll install is a lift up that hill.' He smiled,
then pointed to a cantilevered steel foot-bridge that
spanned the river. 'At least we don't have to row across;
the cabin's on the other side.'

The older man led the way to the bridge. The structure
was some four feet above the surface of the water and
bedded in concrete approaches on both sides. The bank on
the far side was grassy. Some hundred yards beyond and
facing the river stood a substantial, single-storied log
house surrounded by a wide covered verandah. Peregrine
had been expecting something a good deal more primitive.
'Is this the site of the Treaty Ceremony, sir?' he asked as

they crossed the greensward.

'Exactly right, my boy; where we are now. There'll be a fair crowd. I receive Mongo Joyce on the verandah – a latter-day invention as you'll imagine, but it gives everyone a better view.' O'Hara glanced at his watch. 'Now, you'll have time for five hours shut-eye. Place isn't exactly equipped for a long stay – we use it chiefly for picnics – but it has the usual conveniences and I can offer you a bed and some blankets. You'll notice it's a lot cooler up here. I'll give you a shout at six-thirty, I'm always awake then. You'll just need to follow the tow path to Mass, and there's a free breakfast afterwards so you won't starve.' They stepped up on to the verandah. Before opening the door of the cabin O'Hara pointed to the left. 'There's the most marvellous view of the Falls from the end there – right outside your bedroom window. Just below there's a rock stairway down to the bottom – my grandfather had it cut, but it's an even steeper climb than the one we made on the other side.' He was still breathing heavily.

Glen Dogwall's family had originated in the Deep South: he had just been forcefully reminded of traditional prejudices. His stomach still ached from the blow, but his pride had been hurt more than his body. The specific forms of revenge he plotted against Mongo Joyce encompassed everything from physical mutilation to character assassination. In a more sober state he would have planned the order of retributive acts if only to ensure that the Chief Minister would not be so racked by pain as to be spared the full consciousness of his social obliteration. As it was, Dogwall gave his imagination an entirely free rein and felt better by the minute.

The American approached the guest-house by the path that skirted the sea-shore. As he drew close he heard voices. He checked the time, recalling the instructions he had given his wife. The hope blossomed in his mind that some tactical advantage might have been gained after all from what so far had proved a largely unrewarding

evening. If things had gone as planned he should shortly
be in a position to play the outraged husband – the bathroom episode had given him the idea. If it could be alleged
that young Mr Gore had forced his attentions on the unprotected Mrs Dogwall, that should go some part of the
way to spoiling the image of the British contingent with
'Holy' Joe O'Hara. It should also help to ruffle the dignity
of that puffed-up Governor as well as to upset Mr Mark
Treasure – no doubt a pillar of moral rectitude as well as of
the British banking system.

Dogwall liked to think of himself as a simple man. In
truth, only someone as ingenuous as he could have hoped
to carry off such a transparently contrived machination as
one that featured Mrs Dogwall playing the innocent to
advances from Peregrine Gore. The lady herself had been
prompted to express precisely this view but had thought
better of it. She had not achieved the status and comfort
of being the second Mrs Dogwall through failing to co-
operate – and besides, she had found the prospect of a little
licensed dalliance with Peregrine wholly attractive. It
should be added that Glen Dogwall the Third would not
have been President of the Sunfun Hotel Corporation of
America if Glen Dogwall the Second had not been the
founder, the Chairman and the owner of most of the
stock.

The swimming pool area was ablaze with light, a
circumstance that immediately illuminated the fact that
Dogwall was not coming upon a scene of unbridled
abandonment. His wife, decently attired in a short beach
jacket, was sitting at the poolside relaxed and unmolested.
She appeared to be earnestly engaged in conversation
with the man seated beside her. Whatever the stranger's
role and intentions, it was perfectly plain that Mrs Dogwall was in no immediate danger of being ravaged.

The visitor was about Dogwall's own age, but short and
wiry. He was immaculately turned out in a well-tailored,
dark, double-breasted blazer, white trousers and a
yachting cap. The nautical aura was enhanced by a trim

goatee beard. He was holding a tall drink in one hand and a long cigar in the other.

'Hi, honey – meet Paul O'Hawa; he's Joe's bwother visiting from Flowida.'

O'Hara got out of his chair and advanced on Dogwall with almost threatening alacrity. He set down his drink en route and grasped the American's hand. 'Pleased to know you, Dogwall.' The tone was clipped; the manner brisk. 'Sorry to call at this time of night but we've business to discuss that won't wait. Take a chair. Want a drink?' The bustling little man with the darting eyes was already making his host feel like a visitor in his own temporary domain. The question about refreshment was rhetorical since Dogwall was given no opportunity to reply. 'My brother's dotty – you know that – well, you've met him so you must know.' O'Hara, seated again, took a deep pull on his cigar.

'Oh, Joe seems to me . . .' Dogwall's intended cautious defence of Joe O'Hara's sanity was nipped in the bud.

'What he seems is a harmless buffoon. What he is hardly bears analysis.' O'Hara had interrupted without apology. 'He thinks he controls this island and everybody on it – body and soul. Well, he's played God long enough. His latest plan will bankrupt everybody – including me. That's why I'm here. Why don't you sit down?'

Dogwall did as he was bidden. 'But the Sunfun project . . .'

'Is a blind, a front, a come-on, my dear fellow. D'you really think my brother intends to see this island overrun by your greasy tourists?'

In ordinary circumstances Dogwall would have protested at this not entirely inaccurate description of the bulk of Sunfun clients. As it was, he was too alarmed at the import of what he had heard to cavil over niceties. 'Your brother has given me a clear indication . . .'

'If I may say so, the trouble with you Americans is you can't tell a clear indication from a stinking red herring. My brother wants everyone in earshot to think he's

backing your vulgar cause so that he'll have the other lot
begging even to get a hearing. Then he'll administer the
coup de grâce – cunning devil.' O'Hara raised his peaked
cap, wiped the head-band with a white silk handkerchief,
looked up at the sky as though he expected rain, and
rammed the cap back on his head. 'You're bait, Dogwall,
bait – and you're just about to be swallowed whole.'

'I don't think I follow . . .'

The visitor offered an expression indicating that Dogwall had nothing to fear as a follower so long as Paul
O'Hara was leading. 'Then let me make the whole thing
crystal clear. Am I to understand that your real interest
here is in establishing hotels and a casino – that the cigar
business is incidental?'

'You could say that, sure – but the tobacco company is
pretty profitable . . .'

'It won't be from the day after you acquire it – of that
I can assure you.' O'Hara took a long pull at the cigar
he was smoking. 'Stick to Havanas – I always do.'

'You mean . . . ?'

'I mean there's a tiny wrinkle to the King Charles
cigar business that'll get ironed out if ever the company
changes hands. Don't ask me to enlarge because I'm not
going to. Just take my word for it, the business would be
a poor investment at any price.' O'Hara gazed at Dogwall
steadily for a few seconds before continuing. 'I believe
you could still make a packet here out of your sort of
tourism, and I'm ready to help you do it. First, though,
you have to see Joe and withdraw entirely from the
present negotiations.'

'Withdraw . . .'

'Entirely. There's not a cat in hell's chance of your
offer being accepted anyway, so you've nothing to lose.
But with you out of the way Joe has no leverage with this
other bunch. He likes their scheme but not the size of it.
He's hoping to get them to enlarge it, and to buy a minority
interest in O'Hara Industries at an inflated price.'

Dogwall looked disconcerted. 'But he hasn't offered us a

piece of the Company. We might be interested . . .'

'Listen, Dogwall, in no circumstances would Joe offer you anything more than what's been required to get you here. Understand, he doesn't want you except as evidence of competition to other people. But if he commits this island to growing sugar and distilling rum he's on to slow earnings and a seriously reduced income for several years. That's why he needs a slug of capital at the start to keep all his pet projects going. There's another . . . er, personal reason too.'

'He's a sick man.' It was Mrs Dogwall who unexpectedly interjected this conclusion.

'That's very perceptive of you, Mrs Dogwall.'

'Not weally. He had twouble making the stairs after dinner.' Earlier in her life Rachel Dogwall had become quite practised at guessing the physical capacities of older men by the way they managed staircases.

'He's had two heart attacks. The next one . . .' O'Hara shrugged his shoulders.

'But if I withdraw the Sunfun offer, and the other outfit doesn't go for the pricier deal, that's stalemate.' It was Dogwall's turn to demonstrate perception.

'Temporarily, yes.' O'Hara was pleased the American had reached this conclusion on his own. 'Later – I'll tell you when – you come back with another offer, not involving the cigar business. Your present deal is to lease the land around the Rollover Bay area, right?' Dogwall nodded. 'So, your new offer will be to buy a smaller piece of the land – but to buy it outright at a very fancy price and for a strictly limited development.'

'How limited?'

'One hotel, a few expensive cottages.'

'No golf-course . . . ?'

'No golf-course, no casino – but you'll get them and the rest of the land in time. I give you my word on that – and you can have it in writing if it'll make you feel better.' O'Hara smiled. 'One day I'll sell you the whole damned island if you want it – when the featherbedding stops and the people here have to stop living off my family's hand-outs. Meantime, Joe needs some hard cash – more than he's asking for the cigar company.'

'He doesn't look that hard-up to me,' Dogwall put in suspiciously.

O'Hara took a long draw on his cigar. 'He wants to create endowment funds for some of his charities. At the moment he keeps them going out of income. He suspects that when I . . .'

'You inhewit fwom your bwother, Mr O'Hawa?' The enquiry came quite naturally from Mrs Dogwall who had put similar questions to several putative heirs-apparent before settling for the Dogwall matrimonial bed.

'In a word – everything, Mrs Dogwall. The difference is that instead of holding most of it in trust, like my brother I shall be in control.' He glanced at Dogwall to ensure the point had been taken. 'Oh, Joe can dispose of his own creations – like the cigar company – and a limited amount of land. He can also sell up to twenty-four per cent of the holding company – that's O'Hara Industries. Otherwise though, he's stymied. Our father arranged things that way when it was clear Joe was heading for enduring bachelor-hood and would so spoil the family tradition as to die without an heir.' The speaker paused before adding, 'I'm not married myself at the moment – no children either, but there's time enough for all that.' He smiled blandly. Mrs Dogwall regarded the speaker appraisingly, transfer-red her gaze to her husband, and back again to O'Hara.

'Your brother's not up at the house?' Dogwall was unconcerned with Paul O'Hara's marital arrangements.

'No, he's not. He's gone off to his eyrie at Devil's Falls dressed up like Baden-Powell in preparation for the Treaty charade at nine. If you want to beard him early he's always up by seven.' O'Hara continued encouragingly, 'I could probably arrange a car to take you most of the way – but you might find it more comfortable and possibly quicker to walk.'

'Oh, I don't think I'll be rushing any fences.' For the

first time since the conversation began Dogwall was doing his own thinking. 'I guess I'll chew over what you've been saying, O'Hara, and then maybe get with Joe later in the day.'

'Suit yourself. I've told you the score.' O'Hara was not attempting to hide his irritation. He pulled at his beard. 'You're being had and the sooner you call Joe's bluff the more real progress you'll make.' He stood up, swallowed what was left of his drink, and made to leave. 'I've told you where to find Joe if you change your mind – just follow the road or the river path up to the Falls. You can't miss the cabin, it overhangs the Falls.' The directions would hardly have been adequate for a total stranger. It was almost as though it was more important to O'Hara that he should recite them than that they should be understood. 'Now I'll wish you good-night. I hope you'll act on what I've said.' O'Hara moved with energy and speed: he disappeared in the direction of the beach and the path further along that led directly to Buckingham House.

Dogwall stared enquiringly at his wife. 'What you make of that?'

'I make a guy who's playing both ends against the middle, honey, and someone who doesn't have anybody's intewests in mind 'cept his own. He sure wants to keep that cigar company in the family. Hey, d'you know the time? C'mon, let's hit the sack.'

Thus with creditable insight Mrs Dogwall ended the most interesting conversation Sarah had ever overheard from her vantage point on the flat roof of the guest-house.

CHAPTER X

'Is that all of it? It's tiny – and so beautiful. Oh darling, why don't we just buy it for us?' Molly Treasure's first sighting of King Charles Island in the mid-morning sun was eliciting a good deal more enthusiasm than that recorded by Columbus the Younger.

'Because whole islands don't come cheap,' Treasure answered wryly.

'What's that? – it looks like a volcano.' Mount Manitou had registered its presence in the middle distance.

'It is a volcano – classified as a quiet, not explosive type.'

'I'll take your word for it.' The enthusiasm was waning perceptibly.

'It just gives off sulphurous gases – through the crater and fissures down the slope. You can probably take hot sulphur baths; very health-giving.'

'No, you take them. I'm healthy enough. Oh, look, there's a little sea-port.'

'That's Rupertstown, the capital – towns here don't come any bigger.'

'Can you ask the driver – the pilot, I mean – if we can fly all round the island before we land?'

The Treasures had intended to take the regular afternoon flight from Montego Bay where they had spent the night. After two busy days in a wintry New York, an evening under the stars in the warmth of the Caribbean had been sheer luxury. Their plan to laze the morning away on the beach of the Half Moon Hotel had been scotched when they learned over dinner that January 30th was Carnival Day on KCI. At first, Treasure had been irritated that so elementary a piece of intelligence had not reached him sooner. He had every imaginable statistic about the island. He knew the size of the gross domestic product, the state of the trade balance, the value of the staple crops, the extent of the rainfall – even the number of births in and out of wedlock, but no one had thought to tell him that he had planned his arrival to take place on a public holiday.

Like most Englishmen, Treasure viewed public holidays observed abroad and not in Britain with a certain amount of resentment and as evidence of foreign indolence. Whatever the facts of the matter, it always appeared to him – as to most of his compatriots – that foreigners indulged themselves far too frequently with official days off, a practice actually offensive to the Anglo-Puritan work ethic so deeply embedded in the consciousness of a once-proud island race. It was also especially galling that the annual output per worker in the countries most affected by this particular form of inertia was usually better than that obtaining in Britain.

Treasure had thus been doubly affronted at the news about King Charles Day, and had it not been for his wife would have been satisfied perversely to remain in Jamaica doing nothing for the rest of the day rather than journey to KCI to pursue the same purpose.

Molly Treasure had, in contrast, been delighted at the prospect of joining in a fiesta. It was to satisfy this whim that Treasure had chartered a special plane to fly them to Rupertstown in the morning instead of waiting for the later scheduled flight. The cost had been only marginally less resistible than Molly's entreaties, and he wished he had not been so careless as to admit the fact – especially at such length. While they had been waiting at the airport his wife had conjured up a fellow traveller equally anxious to obtain prompt passage to KCI and more than willing to pay a third of the cost of hiring the three-passenger air taxi. Thus Treasure had only his expressed but invented parsimony to blame for having his privacy invaded. He had quite naturally refused the proffered contribution to costs – an action it had given Molly great satisfaction in declaring a manifestation of the worst kind of contrariness.

The grateful and embarrassed extra passenger – a Mr Brown – was seated in front of the Treasures in the co-pilot's seat.

Molly had earlier whispered to her husband that it was proper Brown should be afforded the best all-round view because he had only one eye. He was quite a small man, but it was not until he had actually seated himself that she was satisfied the somewhat cramped quarters at the front of the little single-engined plane would be large enough to accommodate his obviously artificial leg. Treasure's own interest had been limited to speculation about why this battered, be-wigged and worried-looking Englishman should be making a lonely and urgent pilgrimage to KCI: it would not have occurred to him to ask.

Treasure leant forward and tapped the pilot on the shoulder. 'Can we take a spin round the island before we land?'

'Afraid not, sir,' came the reply. 'I can take you up the east coast and back again but the authorities here don't allow overflying to the west. They've got a bird sanctuary that side.' The young pilot smiled. 'In fact they're trying to get guano deposits built up again on Gull Rock – some hope, I'd say. Let me talk to the control tower.' He reached for the switch of his radio transmitter.

'Look, you can see the town's all dressed up.' Molly tugged at Treasure's arm and pointed through the window at Rupertstown below them.

'Mm, there doesn't seem to be much activity, though. I can't see any people.'

Molly glanced at her watch. 'It's only half past nine. They're probably all having breakfast,' she observed firmly.

Treasure was more amused than convinced by this unchallengeable but somehow unlikely conclusion.

'Sorry, we've been told to circle back and come straight in.' This was the pilot. 'The traffic controller sounds pretty agitated – the strip's officially closed.' He banked the plane to the right, away from the shore, and began a wide sweep which was to bring the aircraft in once more over the town but this time on a descent path to the airstrip which lay behind.

'D'you suppose we're staying in Georgian splendour or Strawberry Hill Gothic?'

Treasure followed his wife's gaze. Government House and Buckingham House really did provide a contrast in styles as they came into view on the starboard side of the aircraft. 'Hm, I think you'll be playing Scarlet O'Hara rather than Jane Eyre – but, of course, it's the KCI O'Haras who'll be living in that Gothic monstrosity.'

'How confusing – but I'm glad. The airport's minute.'

The pilot made a perfect landing and taxied the plane towards the long, open-sided building that did duty as KCI's airport complex.

The Treasures disembarked on to the entirely deserted tarmac. Brown followed, looking bewildered. Molly gave him an encouraging smile – the equivalent of the pat she would have applied to a lost dog.

'If you'd all like to follow the sign to customs and immigration I'll see if I can raise a porter for the baggage.' The pilot offered this in a half apologetic tone. 'I guess nobody's working today who doesn't have to, and this flight wasn't scheduled.' He gazed around at the apparently empty airport. 'We did get clearance before leaving Jamaica . . .' He stopped in mid-sentence.

The dark blue Land-Rover came skidding around the corner of the building. It halted dramatically between the parked aircraft and the entrance to the customs area – so dramatically that the engine stalled. Three policemen tumbled out of the vehicle with much clattering of heavy boots and rifle butts.

'Where you from? You from Cuba?' The older of the three African Carleons – a sergeant – barked his question in a clipped, barrack-square manner. 'Stand still.' This last order was directed at the thoroughly frightened Mr Brown who had turned and was limping back to the aircraft.

'Don't be daft, Sammy, we're from Mo'bay where we always come from. I got clearance an hour ago, before take-off. Why the reception committee?' The pilot obviously knew the sergeant, who looked at once irritated and confused at being addressed in such a familiar way.

'I got my orders, Mr Scott. There's no flight scheduled for now, and the airport's officially closed.' The policeman relaxed a little. 'Don' you know there's a state of emergency, man?'

Treasure stepped forward. 'No, we didn't know, Sergeant, and perhaps you'd tell that constable to point his rifle in a less dangerous direction. My name is Treasure and this is my wife. We're here as guests of the Governor.' He avoided making any reference to Brown who was no responsibility of his but who nevertheless was patently not the vanguard of a Communist invasion force. 'We've arrived earlier than we were expected which is why we're not being met.' The first part of this statement was true and the second was a reasonable assumption given that Sir Archibald Rees afforded his guests the elementary courtesies. 'Now, d'you mind telling us what all this is about?'

The sergeant sighed and slung the rifle he was carrying over his shoulder. 'Well, it's like dis, sah. There's bin an assassination. Our mos' respected and bes' loved citizen, Mr Joseph O'Hara, has been brutally beheaded.' Molly Treasure winced. 'Sorry, ma'am. De whole population is on de track o' dat killer.'

'You know who it is?' Treasure put the question.

'Yes, sah, he was caught in de act but he gone escaped. De criminal's name is Perry Green Gore, and when we catch dat man we'll tear him apart.'

It was one of those maturing moments in life when engulfing awfulness proves reality can be worse than nightmares. Peregrine Gore was not without previous experience in this connection but this was the first time he had become a wide-awake victim while crouching in his underpants in the centre of a sugar plantation. Within earshot were a score at least of people intent not simply on catching him but on dismembering him when they had achieved their fairly easy objective.

Already he was regretting he had not stood his ground at the beginning of the whole ghastly episode. That he had failed to do so had probably been an error of judgement but it would have taken more than simple courage to have tested the theory.

It had been eight o'clock when Peregrine had come awake with a start. A glance at his watch confirmed that he had overslept – and that Joe O'Hara had done so too. He was the more angry with himself because he had been awake – or more accurately had been awakened – much earlier, as dawn was breaking. The time had been 5.30 and he had self-indulgently estimated he could slumber on for another hour at least. He remembered concluding that Joe O'Hara must have risen earlier than expected and that the older man could thus be relied upon to rouse him as arranged.

Resigned to the fact that he was too late to set off for the service on Mount Manitou, Peregrine had wandered sleepily from his room into the central area of the log cabin – a large sitting-room giving directly on to the verandah through wide double doors. He had been a little surprised to note that these were open – as was the door to the room he knew O'Hara had been using. It had occurred to him that his host might have risen and gone about his business, having forgotten Peregrine's existence. If this had been so the young man would have been neither surprised nor affronted; if his talents were modest it was to his credit that his disposition and expectancies were also. But he had not been put out of mind by O'Hara – for the sight that had greeted his tentative peek into the older man's room proved that O'Hara no longer had a mind to exercise in any context.

The head had been completely severed from the body. It was this grotesque fact that had registered first – unreal and unbelievable but not, on the instant, as shocking as it was incredible. O'Hara who had been a whole man had become two lifeless objects, not so much separated as seeming to be unassembled – like a shortly to be completed figure at a waxworks. There had been very little blood. The body was lying on a day bed under a long open window. From the thick woollen socks up to the lanyard and neckerchief held in place by the traditional leather woggle – incongruously, Peregrine had recalled the name of this equipage – the figure of a properly uniformed, vintage scout-master had lain in natural repose. The head that should have been resting on a dark blue cushion was propped up in profile on the window ledge; the gaze – appropriately melancholic – appeared to be directed at the curved machete that lay on the same ledge before it.

Peregrine had hurried to the window. The harshest fact he had ever needed to face had not yet been fully accepted by a mind still in need of sleep. There had been no logic – only a strange sense of compassion – involved in his putting out his hands to the severed head, in his lifting it to make sure . . . irrationally to be certain. He had put the cold object down again with a shudder. His gaze had fallen on the stubby cleaver. The blade was clean – but it should not have been. The sabre true cut cleanly through . . . He picked it up.

'Murder!'

The cry had come from a woman. He had looked up and found himself staring through the unglazed window at a dozen or so apparently transfixed Carib warriors dressed in loin-cloths and feathered head-dresses. They were carrying spears. The single woman in the party had on a flowered sarong; she had been carrying a basket. They had all come from the direction of the bridge. Of course, they were the first arrivals for the re-enactment of the Treaty Ceremony – hence their appearance and the antique, ornamental weaponry. Peregrine had consciously regretted that a woman had been obliged to witness the macabre sight. He had been about to instruct one of the men on what should be done when the first ornamental spear demonstrated it did service as the real thing by grazing his shoulder: the natives were no longer transfixed.

'Murderer! Murderer! He kill Uncle Joe.'

The cry had been taken up. More figures had come racing from the bridge. The accusation had been preposterous. The people had no idea of the true facts of the situation. Simply, they had seen Peregrine put down the head – and handle the machete. Another spear had bedded

itself with a thud below the window. Its owner, making up
in enthusiasm what he lacked in practice, was following in
its wake with a cutless in his hand more primitive than the
blade on the window-sill – it was bigger and looked much
more lethal.

'Kill him. We kill him now.'

The mass irresponsibility had been indefensible – like
Peregrine. He had grasped the machete; perhaps a show of
strength . . . ? The crowd had not been impressed. The
leading members had been heaving themselves over the
balcony rail when he had slammed the window shutters
together, inadvertently propelling the head of the late Joe
O'Hara into the advancing throng. There had been a roar
of horror and disgust from outside – quite understandable
in the circumstances, but Peregrine had been in no position to consider niceties. He had plunged back through the
cabin to his own room.

His first intention to gather some of his belongings had
been abandoned as the shouts from outside came ap-
preciably closer. He kept going – through the window,
across the verandah. He dropped the machete on the way.
He had vaulted the balustrade before remembering the
overhang. The drop was twenty feet – with a fine view of
the waterfall, if one had time to appreciate it.

He fell into some light scrub and had rolled thirty yards
downhill before his progress was arrested by a stout tree.
His descent had been parallel with the steps Joe O'Hara's
grandfather had arranged at the side of the Falls; of more
immediate import, his unlikely course had not been
observed by his pursuers. A quick glance upwards confirmed that he was beyond the view of anyone at the cabin.
Eschewing the steps that followed a curving and leisured
route to the river valley, he slipped and tumbled on down
the slope through the brush cover. He was shoeless, more
than half naked, badly scratched, but now fully awake.

At the bottom he had been tempted to hurl himself into
the fast-flowing river to his left – to swim with the current
and to use the cool water as balm for torn skin, as relief

from the painfulness of going further on bare feet. The roar of the waterfall obliterated all other sound but already he could see figures gathering and dispersing, hunting and gesticulating on both sides of the water on the plateau above. A wall of sugar cane to the right had offered the best chance of concealment. He had forced his way into the plantation and pushed onwards at right angles to the river through line upon line of canes.

He had been halted by a high wire fence – a somehow unexpected obstacle. Praedial larceny was surely not rife among the sugar canes. The mesh was a climbable ten feet – but topped by several rows of barbed wire, threaded taut through arched stanchions.

There was no going backwards. He began to pick up the voices of the hunters – it was only a matter of time. The cries were demoniac. Clearly responsible authority was not yet on hand to control an ugly and recognizably blood-thirsty mob – nor, in compensation, to organize a meth-odical search.

It was while Peregrine considered his next move, sitting on the ground and calculating expected events, that the unexpected happened. There was a sudden frenzied rustling behind him, and before he had time to turn there came a quick snort of triumph and something hot, wet and fleshy was thrust into the small of his back.

CHAPTER XI

Sarah, the maid, sat dejected and uncomforted on the bed in her little room at the guest-house. She picked at a tea-towel as big tears coursed down her cheeks. The towel had been set aside for mending but she was mindlessly making the hole in it a good deal bigger.

The source of Sarah's distress was that she had seen a murder – or as good as seen it – a disturbing enough event for any young girl, and the more so for one already involved in an emotional crisis.

Like most Carleons, Sarah had loved Joe O'Hara. He had been a father figure to her. Her mother had been somewhat vague about the identity of her real father. This is not to suggest that by any stretch of imagination or fact Joe could have been the man in question. Simply, there was a question – a common enough one in the West Indies where marriage tends for the underprivileged to feature as an act of capitulation associated with middle age. Despite the Church's influence, King Charles Island was very little different from its neighbours in this respect.

Sarah had been her mother's tenth child – a coincidental tribute to Catholic teaching in one respect at least. However, it cannot be overlooked that nine months previous to the birth Sarah's mother had been co-habiting with three men – not strictly all at the same time, since each had his allocated days of the week. For this reason, it had not been possible accurately to name Sarah's father, a circumstance further confused by the fact that when the child was old enough to utter her first 'Dadda' the three, as it were, certified contenders for the title had been replaced in her mother's affections by three others with no title whatsoever.

It is necessary fully to comprehend these vexing circumstances in order to appreciate the depth of Sarah's transferred but true filial devotion to Joe O'Hara, whose name had featured in virtually every benefaction she had received from infancy upwards and who, by extension, had provided much that a good father should. While it must be admitted this worthy sentiment could properly be shared by all those in the population of KCI in the least mindful of the source of their relative good fortune, for Sarah – an incorrigible romantic – her affection was deepened by a tenuous, remote, but for her very real relationship of a more literally familiar kind.

In the register of St John's Church, Rupertstown, it was recorded for all to see who cared to take the trouble – and Sarah had – that on 1 June 1860, one Maria Josephine

Rafferty, aged seventeen and ten months, had been law-fully married to Matthew James Michael O'Hara, aged seventy-two – despite the almost indecipherable squiggle that recorded this last fact. No more than three days later there was witnessed in that same register the baptism of an infant by the union – one Terence Matthew Michael O'Hara. Old Matthew had been taking no chances in this, as in countless other attempts, to secure a legitimate heir to succeed to his riches and his planned new house.

While there were no less than three hundred souls who were or who claimed to be Raffertys on KCI, and thus the same number who could aspire to some kind of kinship with the O'Haras, it was one whose provable claim in this context was certainly more suspect than most who held it the dearest. Her name was Sarah Rafferty and she was just seventeen years old.

Sarah, who was weeping now, had been near to tears the night before when she had literally eavesdropped on the callous conversation between the Dogwalls and Paul O'Hara – the latter long since established with the islanders as no true Carleon.

It was then that Sarah had finally resolved to emulate the example of the girl she fondly imagined to be her great-great-aunt – or cousin at the very least – and offer herself as a chaste vessel for the carriage of another over-due O'Hara heir. After what she had heard, it seemed to her even more unthinkable than it had been before that Joe was childless by design and not through fault of trying: she would explain he was welcome to try her without obligation.

Having spent some time in prayer, bathed herself and donned a white dress – the symbolism was as convenient as considered; it was her best dress – she had set out for Devil's Falls before dawn. To her credit she had no experience in such matters, but observation in her mother's one-roomed home suggested that elderly men were most disposed to energetic amatory involvement following a night's rest.

On arrival at O'Hara's cabin, Sarah's nerve had failed. It is not, after all, every day that young girls offer themselves in supreme sacrifice to men over sixty, and while, as many male sexagenarians will attest, the probability of rebuff is broadly speaking remote, a girl as innocent as Sarah might understandably have maidenly pause for thought on this count

It was while Sarah was pausing – and well concealed among some bushes beside the cabin – that in the half light of early dawn she saw a man she immediately identified – a respected figure – cross the verandah and enter the house. This man undoubtedly might have proper cause to call upon Mr O'Hara at any time of the day or night, and there was nothing stealthy in the approach. Sarah had wished she had arrived earlier, and with a heavy heart expected to see the two men emerge together – perhaps to make an early start for Mount Manitou. Already she began to plan some other occasion when it might be convenient for Mr O'Hara to have her offer herself to him; she had to take account of how busy he was. Perhaps . . .

It was then that she heard the thud and soon after that the terrible, unbelievable, devil work took place. The man put the head on the ledge not fifty feet from where Sarah was hiding – the severed head of Joseph O'Hara, father of a people, and more particularly, until lately prospective father of Sarah Rafferty's first-born. It had been all Sarah could do not to cry out – not to vent the scream that welled in her throat. But she had somehow kept silent. In truth, fears for her own safety overcame all other considerations, though still she could not credit that the man who next stole away from the cabin would do her harm – even after what she had witnessed.

In horror she had fled the scene. All thoughts of attending Mass on the mountain went from her mind – the Mass she had intended would sanctify her union with the great man and bring God's blessing on a conception as immaculate as Maria Josephine Rafferty's in 1860, which, as it happened, had been nothing of the sort.

Sarah picked at the tea-cloth and mourned the loss of her divinely appointed role. Soon she would mourn a little for Joe O'Hara too. After that it was reasonable to expect she would come to think about her public responsibility; she was only seventeen, and very romantic.

The curious-looking pig flopped on to its haunches and fixed Peregrine with a baleful stare. Most members of the pig species affect an air of disenchantment; this one was especially lack-lustre after establishing through touch and smell that Peregrine was not one of her own kind.

Peregrine was only relieved at the sight of the harmless intruder and not conscious that his bare flesh had just been inspected for pig-like propensities. He stared back at the creature which, while continuing to fix her eyes on his, began swaying her head from side to side in mournful negation.

Pigs, Peregrine was dimly aware, came in a variety of colours, shapes and sizes. The example here presented corresponded only in a few particulars to the sorts he had observed on farms; indeed, the short tusks suggested it might properly belong in a zoo. Then again, it seemed a friendly enough creature; the tusks were really only protruding back teeth, and, despite the long snout and bristly mane, the dark brown body and floppy ears had a woolly, cuddly look. There was also the evidence of the mournful countenance.

At the turn of the century, Terence O'Hara's ceaseless efforts to find cross breeds of livestock suited to the environment of KCI had produced stranger hybrids than the kind now confronting Peregrine. The *Sus scrofa*, or wild boar of Southern Europe, the Large Black and other strains of Chinese origins had all played their parts. The young gilt-pig breathing heavily on Peregrine's knee was sufficiently unique not to merit connection with any registered Breed Society; it was literally a reject and actually a throw-back. Not surprisingly, it was also lonely.

Peregrine extended a hand and tentatively gave the pig a pat on the head. The animal promptly rolled over on its back, exhibited an ample stomach and gave a grunt that was unmistakably one of pure pleasure. Peregrine had made a friend – and one which by instinct appeared to recognize that one good turn deserved another.

The pig heaved itself on to its feet, swayed a little, and then proceeded a few yards along the wire fence with a gait that was noticeably unsteady. It paused and slowly turned its head as though to ensure that Peregrine was following. Since, so far as the fugitive was concerned, one direction was as good as another, he complied; the pig proceeded, from time to time bumping into the fence, and several times falling over. Had the creature been human Peregrine would have had no hesitation in concluding that it was inebriated – but a drunken pig was hard to credit.

Peregrine glanced behind him; there was no sign of pursuit. On looking ahead once more he observed a fundamental change in the order of progress. The pig was now on the other side of the wire, and while, earlier, the two had been following a beaten if not actually well-trodden path, the way ahead for Peregrine was now overgrown and undisturbed. Clearly the path – or what there was of it – had crossed the wire; any hole or tunnel capable of taking a pig two feet high and broad withal would certainly accommodate Peregrine. He retraced his steps. The clean-cut gap in the fence might be convenient for a pig, but it had been made by human hand. Peregrine squeezed under the wire without difficulty.

The companionable pig had fallen over again, and this time was showing no inclination to pick itself up and proceed. It lay stretched out on its back emitting short and regular grunts of a kind that might easily have been taken for snores: there was no mistake – the pig had gone to sleep.

Peregrine debated whether he should go on alone. It was at once absurd and humiliating to have one's movements dependent on the whims of a narcoleptic pig – casually encountered and of questionable sobriety. On the other hand, the pig alone knew the terrain, and before its collapse had evidently been purposefully heading for some firm objective – perhaps a human habitation.

Assuming there remained some rational beings on the island ready to accept a chap's account of his innocence before exacting summary retribution on a guiltless stranger, human habitation equipped with a telephone was what Peregrine most sought. The probability that the pig was someone's bizarre pet had already occurred to him: the creature behaved more like a dog than a farmyard outcast, and anyone who had developed an affection for it almost had to have a better than average sense of compassion.

What semblance of a path had existed beside the fence had ceased abruptly at the point where the pig was taking its ease. The character of the plantation had altered too. On the other side of the wire maturing canes had been standing, rank upon rank. Here, after penetrating some yards beyond the vicinity of the fence – and the pig had done just this – one came upon lines of cane planted nearly twice the distance apart with a different, squatter crop growing in between the rows.

Peregrine had no immediate idea what the short, spreading, small-leafed plants might be. Each was topped by a bud showing yellow at the extremity. Simply, he registered that this was a better husbanded area than the one he had left – all the spare ground had been recently turned over and the pipes of what he recognized as a rudimentary trickle irrigation system were much in evidence.

The pig stirred, blinked at Peregrine, and lumbered to its feet. It shook its head vigorously from side to side as though to attest the sterling recuperative value of forty winks. It next made quick progress into – rather than simply up to – the nearest of the bushy green plants, stretched its short neck as though in flabby emulation of a wolf baying at the moon, and with a heave from its rear quarters succeeded in biting off the yellowing bud at the crown. Still standing inside the bush it devoted itself to the evidently pleasurable task of noisy mastication. Peregrine had fallen in with a flower-eating pig.

Over the next few minutes it became clear that further reliance on the quadruped for guidance could be abandoned. She moved from plant to plant repeating the bud-capturing ritual. This had been her goal – not to return to some doting owner who would provide as sustenance the slops and common fodder that suited the tastes of ordinary pigs.

Peregrine glanced both ways along the line of shrubs the pig was systematically debudding. He then broke from the cover of the sugar cane across to the next row. The pig gave her departing companion a look that might easily have been intended as incredulous, before returning her full attention to the serious business on hand. She seemed to be signifying that if he was spurning the veritable Eden of succulent greenery to which she had led him, then he was no longer any concern of hers.

After traversing a dozen or so of the shrub lanes, Peregrine began to wonder whether he might not be on a fruitless course, penetrating into the heart of some vast plantation. It was while he was considering retracing his steps to the fence, and following this in the hope of coming upon a gate and pathway, that he heard the noise of an internal combustion engine coming to life only a little way ahead. He dived across into the next row of canes, crouched low, and carefully parted the foliage that screened him.

The view was clear across some fifty yards of grassy scrub to a long, squat building served by a railway line that snaked up from a pair of tall gates some distance to the left. But it was the human activity that fixed Peregrine's attention – and immediately raised his hopes for proper sanctuary.

Figures were clustered around two large tractors in the foreground while others were scampering in and out of the open door at the end of the building, feeding the smoking interior of a steel incinerator outside with highly combustible material. Several more members of the industrious little work force were pushing flat rail wagons from one of the two buffered sidings that terminated the line. And what so encouraged Peregrine about the whole scene was that all the figures were white-habited nuns – persons who would have neither the means nor the inclination to hurl spears at him.

The engine Peregrine had heard earlier belonged to one of the tractors which, under the competent control of a diminutive nun, now began to move off across his line of sight towing a twin-bladed hoe. Another nun was clambering on to the driving seat of the second tractor while two others hitched a hoe behind. This task completed, the two scurried over to a manually-operated inspection trolley parked on the railway line, mounted it so that they faced one another, and began propelling it towards the gates by in turn depressing and lifting its operating bars. The little vehicle progressed along the line at a quite surprising speed and to the evident enjoyment of its chattering occupants who looked and behaved as though they were astride a mobile see-saw.

The second tractor emitted several back-fires, then proceeded erratically to follow the tracks of the first, past the belching furnace.

The nuns on the trolley dismounted on reaching the gates, unlocked these, and fixed them open before returning to the marshalling area, propelling their singular conveyance with the same gusto they had demonstrated earlier.

It was the darting figure of the evidently oldest member of the group that Peregrine was most anxious to observe. A large bunch of keys dangled from her waist and she was clearly in charge – some of the time issuing orders, and the rest gliding about busily to assist at the tasks her minions were performing. It was her age as much as her authority that prompted Peregrine to single her out. He hoped that when the others had completed their work they might depart, leaving her alone and more easily approachable.

For although the fugitive was confident he could surrender himself with equanimity here in a civilized community, there remained the embarrassment of his appearance. The single undergarment in which he had made his escape was now very much the worse for wear; not to put too fine a point on it, the thing was in tatters – and no fit raiment in which to enter the sheltered lives of a whole bevy of young nuns.

It was while Peregrine continued to delay his appearance in the hope of a reduced audience that the unexpected happened. The nuns were, indeed, dispersing, more in answer to a summoning bell than because their work was over. After herding her flock away from what they were doing – they formed up in twos and made off towards the rear of the building – Sister Helena (for it was she who had been supervising) consulted her watch and, after a moment's hesitation, began counting the flat wooden packing cases that the pair from the trolley had later turned to stacking on a rail wagon. While she was doing this – her back to the open door – a man's head poked out from behind the threshold.

The newcomer surveyed the scene and then – confirming he was as much an interloper as Peregrine – raced swiftly to the limited shelter of the trolley car. Peregrine immediately recognized the man who was clad in dark shirt and trousers and a black beret pulled down over his ears; he was clutching a small canvas bag: white tennis shoes assisted his surreptitious movements but detracted somewhat from the otherwise apparent attempt at a shadowy camouflaged appearance.

Sister Helena glanced behind her as though conscious of some other's presence. Seeing no one, she continued her count and began straightening a stack of boxes. While she was thus engaged the dark figure broke from cover and made a not very stylish but reasonably timed sprint for the very clump of sugar canes in which Peregrine was concealed.

The fifty-yard dash went unobserved by the preoccupied nun who looked up at the sound – but too late for the sight – of the man's dive into the covering foliage.

'Mr McLush, isn't it?' said Peregrine with a formality hardly justified by the nature of the occasion. 'What are you doing here?'

CHAPTER XII

Sir Archibald Rees rose from his seat at the table in the white-walled Council Room of Government House. Mark Treasure had just entered and was surprised to find the Governor still clad in the denim boiler suit he had been wearing when they had first met earlier – although he had discarded the peaked cap somewhere along the way. Perhaps the man imagined the clothes added a Churchillian flavour to his appearance – in truth, they made him look like an engine-driver.

'We are in a difficult situation,' said Rees. 'This is Chief Inspector Small who's in charge of the Police Force,' he added without making it clear whether this was intended as amplification of his first observation.

In contrast to his name, Eric Small was a robust, amiable-looking Englishman with a country face, like a happy apple. He extended a large hand to Treasure, who discerned a touch of West Country in the baritone greeting. He also noted the Distinguished Service Medal amongst the ribbons on the khaki uniform jacket. 'How d'you do, sir – or rather, glad to see you again.' Treasure affected surprise. 'No, I didn't expect you'd remember me. We only met briefly the last time – a year ago it was. You were the guest speaker at a Police Federation dinner – very witty too, if I may say so.'

Treasure recalled the occasion but not the face. 'How kind of you. But how did you come to be there?'

Rees broke in with a touch of impatience. 'Do sit down, both of you. Small was seconded to us six months ago.'

Treasure did as he was bidden, nodding to Mongo Joyce whom he had met shortly after his arrival an hour before.

It was eleven o'clock. The Treasures had been transported to Government House – conspicuously – in the back of the police Land-Rover. Mr Brown had been left to find his own way to the hotel, and had seemed grateful rather than disaccommodated at the prospect.

It was Lady Rees and her daughter who had first received the guests with – in the circumstances – a creditable display of ceremony. Treasure had been relieved at their joint and firmly expressed belief in Peregrine's innocence, and also at the intelligence that Archie Rees was about to make a special broadcast which would include the same sentiment.

They had been in time to hear the Governor's statement declaring a day of mourning, cancelling the carnival, and suggesting that people should remain quietly at home. The reference to Peregrine had been oblique. Joseph O'Hara's assassin, the speaker reported, had not yet been identified. The police and others were adjured not to mistreat any suspects.

Rees had appeared shortly after the broadcast accompanied by the Chief Minister. The two had asked to be excused for some private consultation, but Treasure had been invited to join them at eleven.

The Governor cleared his throat. 'If I might come to the point, Mr Treasure. We all of us accept that Gore could hardly have been responsible for the murder, but in the circumstances . . . the so-called witnesses, and so on . . .'

Treasure interrupted to relieve the embarrassment. 'I

understand, and of course the chap has a lot of explaining to do, but first we have to find him – and I trust in one piece.'

'He'll be looked after, don't worry.' This was Mongo Joyce. 'People got a bit hot under the collar earlier – they've calmed down now.'

Treasure hoped he was right. 'Who do you think did do the murder?'

Rees answered, 'A vagrant, a thief . . .'

'We can't exclude voodoo,' the Chief Minister interrupted. 'Anyway, it was the work of a very sick mind.'

'Which excludes Gore.' Treasure was anxious to make this point as often as possible. The others nodded. 'I assume the death of Mr O'Hara means that any commercial discussions will eventually be held with his heir. I gather his brother . . .'

'On the contrary, Mr Treasure, they will be held with the elected Government of the island.' Joyce spoke quietly but firmly.

'I should explain,' put in the Governor, 'we've just had a telephone conversation with Paul O'Hara. He has Mr Dogwall with him . . .'

'The Sunfun chap?' Treasure made no attempt to cover his surprise.

'Correct.' Rees looked disconcerted, but continued hurriedly. 'He explained certain plans which the Chief Minister found unacceptable.' Rees hesitated. 'I must say I support Mr Joyce in his attitude . . .'

'What the Governor means is that Paul O'Hara is not taking on the mantle of Joe – no way. Aloysius Babington was speaking as a Carleon . . . for the people.' Joyce had not raised the pitch of his voice.

'I'm sorry, I don't follow.' Treasure was genuinely puzzled.

'Father Babington is our senior resident priest,' Rees offered without emotion. 'At a Mass attended by nearly a thousand islanders this morning he denounced Joe O'Hara for betraying the people and the country. He called for an end to what he named the O'Hara dynasty, and a boycott of the Treaty Ceremony. It really was an unnerving harangue – but courageous in its way.'

'And right. Father Babington is right – more than ever now that Joe's gone,' Joyce put in with acerbity.

'Yes, but he didn't know Joe was dead. At least . . .' The Governor paused theatrically, then shook his head sharply as though to dismiss the unthinkable. 'It's true, Mr Treasure, that the passing of Joe O'Hara most certainly opens the way for a more . . . er . . . a more constitutional approach to the island's affairs. We cannot overlook the symbolic nature of the beheading. The date and . . . er . . . so on.'

'Did the priest say in what way the late Mr O'Hara was betraying the people?' Treasure had an uneasy feeling that his own presence might somehow be involved.

'He didn't need to, Mr Treasure.' This was Joyce again. 'Enough of us knew he intended to sell out to Dogwall.'

'Including young Gore, I gather,' the Governor added, perhaps by way of indicating that Peregrine had not been entirely forgotten.

Treasure ignored the reference to his assistant. He looked towards the Chief Minister. 'That would have been no more in my interest than the island's. Even so, did it deserve a kind of papal denunciation?'

It was the Governor who answered. 'The situation may not be as clear-cut as the Chief Minister here is suggesting. I doubt Babington intended in any sense to align himself with what we might call the constitutionalists. His approach would be pragmatic . . .'

Joyce smiled sourly. 'I'm not suggesting that Aloysius Babington was speaking in support of independence for KCI. He doesn't think along those lines – not yet. Right now he's more concerned stopping causes than dealing with effects.'

'Causes big enough to lead to murder – or a symbolic execution?' Treasure glanced at the Governor.

Inspector Small stirred himself. 'We don't know yet how

Mr O'Hara lost his life, but I'll stake my reputation it wasn't through having his head cut off.'

Sir Archibald Rees nodded – apparently in vigorous agreement.

Aloysius Babington sat staring at his hands in the study of the Presbytery. He had washed only minutes before making the telephone call to the convent; he resisted the compulsion to do so again. What was done was done. The blood that had been on his hands he could picture there still; no ritual cleansing would erase it.

Did he feel remorse? He had asked himself that question a dozen times in the last few hours. The strangely dispassionate answer came to him again: certainly he felt grief, but there was no sense of guilt. What he had done he would do again if circumstances and his own conscience dictated such a course. It was his function to serve the will of God and to protect the people. For so long he had been at one with Joe O'Hara in these worthy aims. Now he would mourn Joe's loss to the end of his days – and steel himself to see that the friend he had considered misguided had not died in vain.

He had already fulfilled Joe's wishes in one respect. His orders to the convent had been to destroy the crop by ploughing in and to burn what was in store. Paul O'Hara's telephone call had not altered this decision. The priest had made one apparent concession to the first blustering, then pleading O'Hara. He had sanctioned the immediate collection of cigars ready for shipment. There had always been a contingency plan – and supply – against an emergency: Sister Helena knew what had to be done.

Thus Babington had kept faith with what had been last agreed with Joe over the cigar business. What he could not credit was Paul's assertion that Joe had never intended to take the Sunfun project any further. If this was so, why had Joe protested the opposite in this very room the day before? Paul called in his brother's strategy to ensure that no one – including Babington – could give away his real intention. The priest reluctantly accepted there were some grounds for the contention remembering how he had inadvertently leaked Joe's earlier confidence to Mongo Joyce. Was it possible his friend had not considered him worthy as a confidant – at least outside the confessional? If only . . .

Babington dismissed a premise too heartbreaking even to consider. Paul was wrong – worse, he was lying in his account of what had come out during the argument he had had with his brother the night before. An alternative conclusion was unthinkable in terms of the priest's own actions – unthinkable and unforgivable. In any event there must be no further delay in pursuing his next considered course. There were circumstances in which the secrecy of the confessional could serve to protect the wrongdoer to no purpose.

Father Aloysius Babington prepared to leave for the police station.

Molly Treasure was not given to inactivity when there was a part available for the playing. Sipping coffee with Debby and Mrs Dogwall in the faded elegance of the drawing-room at Government House had no attraction compared to the plan of action she had just proposed. 'Then what are we waiting for?' she asked firmly. 'Peregrine is bound to know the Morse code,' she continued, and then as though to dismiss the self-doubt that immediately assailed her she added, 'Even I know the Morse code.'

Mrs Dogwall nodded enthusiastically. 'I think it's a tewific idea, Mrs Tweasure. Poor Pewegwine, he's out there somewhere thinking the whole world's against him.'

Molly smiled approvingly. The woman might look common but clearly her heart was in the right place.

Debby Rees wished that Mrs Dogwall had not happened along in time to be included in the Peregrine Gore rescue operation but the situation had to be accepted. 'He's bound to be somewhere on the west of the island. If you think it'll work we can be mobile in ten minutes,' she offered, limping towards the door. 'It's too frustrating sitting here.'

'You're sure you can manage?' asked Molly.

'Absolutely,' Debby answered with an assurance not entirely justified by the pain in her ankle. 'It isn't far, and I know Luke will still be down with the engine.'

In fact it was more Mrs Dogwall's platform-heeled shoes than Debby's disability that slowed the progress of the three women to the railway shed, and it was fifteen minutes before *Sir Dafydd*, driven by a slightly bewildered Luke Murphy, emerged from the yard with the State carriage in tow.

'It's just like Disneyland,' Mrs Dogwall cried as she stepped aboard, exhibiting a delicacy and balance appropriate to embarking on a badly-moored rowing boat.

'Actually it's the other way round,' Debby countered with feeling. 'This is quite an old-established railway and the engine's a collector's piece' – observations that earned her a grimace of approval from the driver who was in earshot of these loud exchanges.

The little train threaded its way over the bridge and through the outskirts of the town on to the cultivated plain beyond. The journey was proving quite as exciting as Molly Treasure had hoped – if a trifle less comfortable. The carriage had no sides, though the four pairs of cushioned, double wooden seats were fitted with arms. As the engine gathered speed the rocking of the whole contraption suggested that unwary passengers might be inadvertently ejected on sharp curves.

'I expect you and your husband do a great deal of travelling, Mrs Dogwall.' Molly offered this by way of polite conversation to the occupant of the seat in front.

'Mm, but not by twain.' The comparison with Disneyland was palling. 'I guess jet airplanes have it over steam engines.'

'Both British inventions,' Debby put in loudly. 'Did your husband enjoy his ride this morning, Mrs Dogwall?'

She was leaning backwards over the front seat. 'Daddy drove the breakfast special up before daylight. He said Mr Dogwall was on board.'

'Oh, he thought it was tewific. He got off half-way 'cos he was jogging back.'

'He was what?' Molly asked.

'Jogging, Mrs Tweasure. Glen wuns evewy morning – even when we're in Chicago. He'd have gone to the Mass, 'cept we're sorta Baptists.'

Molly resisted the temptation to enquire whether the 'sorta Baptists' were affiliated to the Southerns or the Anas. She peered ahead at the cane fields the train was approaching. 'Debby, I think you could ask nice Mr Murphy to start signalling on his whistle. Remind him it's a short, two longs and a short – di-da-da-di.'

'Sounds kinda long for a little letter like p,' said Mrs Dogwall earnestly. 'Gee, I hope Pewegwine weally does know this horse code.'

'Morse code, my dear – and Peregrine was an officer in the Brigade of Guards.' The confidence in Molly's tone conjured up pictures of Peregrine leading calvary charges armed with an Aldis lamp.

Debby shouted her instruction across to Luke Murphy whose following first attempt to make the steam whistle emit anything approximating to the Morse cipher for the letter p was confounded by the vagaries of the ancient mechanism at his command. The first shrill blast came out well enough but its unscheduled isolation was as marked as its intended brevity. Luke primed a recalcitrant valve and tried again. The result, though breathy in parts, was a just distinguishable signal. The third and quickly following fourth renderings were spirited and true. 'Di-da-da-di, di-da-da-di,' went the whistle.

'Deep in the heart of Texas,' sang Mrs Dogwall, off key but demonstrating a singular rhythmic acuity. 'Say, shouldn't we stop the twain now and again? I mean, Pewegwine's never going to catch us' – but he did.

CHAPTER XIII

Treasure filled a pipe while waiting for Chief Inspector Small to finish his telephone conversation. They were seated in Small's office at the Rupertstown Police Station. The modern whitewashed block in the main square behind the harbour was also – on its seaward aspect – the headquarters of H.M. Customs and Excise. In addition, on the way in, Treasure had noted a plaque directing those involved in business with Radio-KCI to ascend to the upper floor and turn left, in contrast to any wishing to pay their telephone accounts who were instructed to follow the same route and to turn right. From all this he concluded he was at the nerve centre of the law, order, and electronically-controlled communication applying on the island.

On the short drive from Government House the Chief Inspector had explained his one year secondment to KCI from the Avon and Somerset Constabulary. The island's Chief of Police was on a senior officer's training course in Britain, and being within a year of retirement Small – a widower – had been glad to volunteer as his temporary replacement.

In general he found the life agreeable and the paramilitary force of thirty men under his command willing if ill-trained. Since crime had been reported non-existent on King Charles he had been looking forward to a quiet sabbatical on full pay. The murder of Joe O'Hara had shaken him more than he cared to own to anyone save Treasure: he was not a CID man and it had been some years since he had been directly involved in a murder investigation.

Small replaced the receiver. He smiled at Treasure. 'Well, the body's reached Kingston, courtesy of Mr Dogwall's jet aeroplane. We should have an autopsy report in a few hours.'

'Of course, there is a hospital here.' Treasure had taken cognizance of this fact before his departure. He tried to avoid visiting communities devoid of proper medical facilities – a habit he regarded as an elementary precaution; his wife called it hypochondria.

Small nodded. 'Two doctors. Nice chaps. One's on leave in Canada and the other went down with food poisoning yesterday.' Treasure made a mental note to avoid the local water, unwashed fruit, and undercooked meat; more elementary precautions. Small continued. 'I doubt either of 'em would have been too keen about doing this particular post-mortem. Anyway, it was I who suggested Jamaica, and the Governor agreed.'

'And Paul O'Hara?'

'Wasn't a bit keen – but I didn't give him the option. It's probably high-handed, but I'm playing this by the book, sir.'

'Quite right, Chief Inspector.' Treasure paused. 'You said earlier you were certain death wasn't caused by the decapitation . . .'

'No blood, not to speak of, that is. Oh, there was a bit – and a lot of mess, of course. But if Mr O'Hara had had his head chopped off while he was still alive there'd have been blood everywhere. Even Father Babington mentioned as much. It was he who put the head in the coffin with the rest of the body.' Small hesitated. 'Strange situation, that was. They were close friends until . . . well, I suppose until Father Babington sounded off at the Mass. Then, when we'd finished at the Falls and I told them to take the corpse away nobody'd touch the head – not the medical orderlies nor my policemen. Was going to do it myself – then the padre stepped forward and picked it up. Very dignified and reverent, he was – but somehow cold with it.'

'Unemotional?'

'That's it. And the crowd knelt – as though it was a funeral service. Lot of people there by that time. Made a big impression on me, that did.' Small reflected for a moment, then looked up sharply. 'I don't mind telling you I'll be glad of any help you can give, sir – you being familiar with the procedures and so on, and not local too.' His eyes twinkled. 'I remember Superintendent Bantree introducing you at that dinner as the best amateur copper in the business.'

Treasure chuckled. 'Colin Bantree and I have cracked more jars than cases – but of course I'll assist in any way possible. You're not going to get CID officers in from Jamaica or London?'

'Certainly not from Jamaica – Carleons have a traditional dislike of anyone official from there poking into affairs here. If we have reason to believe Mr O'Hara was more than the victim of a common assault by some vagrant, then I'll bring in the Yard . . .'

'Reason to believe?' Treasure felt this piece of police jargon was intended to carry a special significance. 'You mean if it appears that a top person with a special motive could be responsible. D'you think that could be?'

Small shrugged his shoulders. 'I hope not, sir. I sincerely hope not. That baccy smells good.'

Treasure pushed his pouch across the desk. 'Help yourself, it's a private mixture from Lewis in St James's.' He frowned. 'I see your point. Of course there aren't many top people in a place like this . . .'

'And not one I'd care to book for speeding, let alone suspicion of a serious crime – not unless it was open and shut, if you see what I mean, sir.'

Treasure took the point. 'Meantime you've taken photos, combed the cabin for evidence . . .'

'Including fingerprints,' the Chief Inspector cut in. 'There were plenty of dabs but those that don't belong to Mr O'Hara and your Mr Gore were probably made – or spoiled – by the rush of outraged citizens. We'll see. Anyway, the place is now locked and cordoned. I've posted a day and night guard so nothing will spoil.' He paused, and then let out a disconsolate sigh. 'Frankly, I don't believe I've got a blooming thing to go on, sir, not so far at least.

If you'd like to look over the cabin yourself I'd be glad to take you up there.'

'Perhaps after we've found Gore.' Convinced as he was of Peregrine's innocence, Treasure deemed it more sensible to stay away from the scene of the crime until that conviction was shared universally. He did not want to be open to a charge of destroying evidence against Peregrine – though if the circumstances and consequences had not been so grave, he reflected bitterly, he might be more in the mood to invent some. 'About the top people?' he asked. 'Any fancied runners?'

The Chief Inspector spent a moment longer than was strictly necessary lighting his pipe. He gave a smile of appreciation. 'Mm, very mellow, sir. There was this dinner-party last night at Government House. On the face of it, only the people there would have known the late Mr O'Hara was intending to sleep at the cabin – them and Mr Paul O'Hara.'

'On the face of it?'

Small shrugged his shoulders. 'He apparently made up his mind to go up to the cabin when he saw his brother's yacht arriving – and said so loud enough for most people to hear. He or any of them could have told others – or the servants might have . . .'

'But you're quite right – it gives us a starting-point, Chief Inspector. D'you know who was there and how they spent the rest of the night?'

'This is a copy of the guest list, so the answer to your first question's easy.' The policeman extracted a paper from the worn leather brief-case he had placed before him on the desk. He handed Treasure the typed sheet.

'Were you there?' the banker asked before glancing down at the list. The question was intended to suggest that the Chief Inspector was as likely and entitled as anyone else to be on dining terms with the Governor. That this was not the case had been more evident from the man's treatment and demeanour at Government House than it was from the fact that his name was not listed. The assumption was nevertheless appreciated.

Eric Small gave a wry smile. 'Not on this occasion, sir, no. I did get invited to lunch once – with the Harbourmaster and the Postmistress, as I recall. There's what you might call a . . .'

'A Governor's pecking order?' Treasure interrupted, and the two men exchanged understanding looks.

'Governor's lady, actually, sir. Probably thinks coppers belong below stairs.'

'Mm. Wonder where she places bank managers?' Treasure purposely completed his levelling tactic. 'Anyway, you didn't know Joe O'Hara was . . . er . . . going up country for the night, which rather makes your point, since you're head of a pretty important grapevine. Of the people who did know . . . let me see now – ' he studied the list – 'who's Mr Angus McLush? Is he a VIP or does he just play the bagpipes after dinner?'

'Journalist, friend of Sir Archibald's.' Small offered the last comment as though to explain why Lady Rees had allowed a reporter over her threshold. 'Odd sort of cove as a matter of fact – what you might call a failed intellectual forced into making a living.' This comment at once covered the Chief Inspector's view of McLush and – by implication – all those whose tutored understanding left them short of Senior Wrangler status. 'Funny you should pick on him because we can't find him.'

'Which suggests you think he's worth looking for?'

'Not me especially – not up to now, that is. No, he gets a salary as the island's information officer – PRO, I suppose you'd call him. Obviously the Governor wanted him toot sweet this morning but he hasn't shown up. We've enquired at his house – he lives alone – and all we've got is that he went out some time after midnight. He woke the little girl in the house next door as he was leaving.'

'Did he get on with Joe O'Hara?'

'That I couldn't say, sir. Mr O'Hara was his employer in an indirect kind of way so it's likely they were on friendly terms.'

'Well, we'll need an account of his movements since midnight when he reappears.' Treasure looked up. 'This not knowing the time of death keeps us in the dark in more ways than one.'

'True, sir. But young Mr Gore should be able to . . . to throw some light on the subject when we find him. He certainly slept at the lodge and since that must have been by invitation chances are he was the last to see Mr O'Hara alive.'

'Last but one,' Treasure put in with a smile. 'At least, we hope so. What about the other people on this list? I suppose they were all innocently tucked up in bed with witnesses during the relevant hours of darkness.'

'Not quite all – and not strictly innocently, I'm afraid, sir.'

Treasure drew in his breath in mock surprise. 'You mean Lady Rees was out on an immoral engagement?'

Small clearly enjoyed savouring this suggestion. 'Nothing so spicy, I'm afraid, nor unlikely. Mr Dogwall was up pretty early – I don't know how early because I haven't asked him, but the Governor told me he was on one of the first trains out. That was the one they call the breakfast special that takes up the food and equipment for feeding the people after the service.'

'And Dogwall was on it?'

'As far as the Gull Rock spur – that's about half-way. According to the Governor who was driving the train, Mr Dogwall got off there and ran . . . er, jogged back.'

'He's not religious – or else he didn't trust the Governor's driving. What time would that have been?'

'Around five fifty-five.'

'Have you met Dogwall?'

'I haven't had that pleasure yet, sir. I met his wife for a minute this morning. Proper bobby-dazzler, she is.'

Treasure considered this might offer more reason for Dogwall to stay in bed than to get up at unconventional hours, but he kept the thought to himself. He glanced again at the list. 'We must assume Father Babington spent the night alone but that if he'd done in O'Hara he wouldn't have bothered denouncing him during the sermon.'

'I'd come to the same conclusion, sir.' Small's tone was matter of fact and indicated that as a good Protestant he had no scruple about assessing the homicidal tendencies of Catholic priests – at least given special circumstances. 'What he said was pretty strong stuff, of course. I was there. He fairly laid into Mr O'Hara.'

Treasure nodded. 'Verbally, at least. Did he also take the train?'

'I don't know, but I wouldn't think so. It's a point of honour, as you might say, with the islanders that the able-bodied walk to this particular service – makes it into a sort of pilgrimage. Mind you, it's quite a step.'

'Past the O'Hara cabin?'

'You can go that way but there are plenty of easier footpaths up this side of the island – less winding than the river path, and not so steep at the end. I drove up myself in a Land-Rover – it being an on-duty occasion.' Small thus indicated that though able-bodied he placed his responsibility as chief crowd controller before any intent to be a pilgrim. 'As things turned out, it was just as well I was mobile. Anyway, there were a good many walkers on the road at six-thirty. I didn't see Father Babington, but whichever route he took he's bound to have fallen in with others.'

Treasure had purposely been bringing up the names of those who by some stretch of imagination or known fact might have had cause to dispatch the murdered man. He wondered whether his next choice from the list might prove to be the butt of the policeman's earlier barb. 'I see the Chief Minister's wife was with him at dinner.'

'As she is on most public occasions.' Small shook his head before continuing. 'He's a good-looking chap – oh, as you saw for yourself.'

'But his bedtime alibi . . .'

'Will either be embarrassing or it'll involve him and

others in a slight case of perjury, sir. He keeps a mistress at the end of the road.'

'How very convenient.'

Small's views on such matters clearly did not run to jocularity. 'It's not exactly common knowledge, more what you might call an open secret. The lady's English, and wealthy by all accounts. I've seen her about – name of Lady Cynthia Franks-Barrett.'

Treasure's eyebrows lifted. 'You're right about the wealth – in terms of the family anyway. They're what might vulgarly be described as rolling in it. And she lives here on the island?'

'A good deal of the time, sir. She has an estate in Jamaica and some sort of establishment in New York. She's unmarried – no chicken, and not much of a looker, come to that.'

'But the Chief Minister is captivated by her riches?'

'That and her liberal views, sir – politically speaking, I mean.'

'I must say you're singularly well informed on this subject.'

'Not me so much as the chap I'm relieving.' Small leant across the desk. 'He gave me a pretty thorough briefing on our Lady Cynthia for obvious reasons. Officially she's a casual visitor and her presence is ignored by everyone from the Governor down . . .'

'And up?'

It took the Chief Inspector a moment to understand Treasure's meaning. 'Oh, Mr O'Hara knew she was about, but I was told he had no knowledge of her relationship with Mr Joyce.'

'Or didn't want to have. This is a pretty small community. I should have thought . . .'

'Exactly, sir.' Small nodded agreement with the implication. 'On the other hand, it's outwardly a very Catholic community. I imagine you have to do penance for gossiping.'

Treasure smiled. He wondered why the reputedly

talented and competent Chief Minister bothered with maintaining a social charade to protect his position on a tin-pot island. If the man was emotionally engaged with a member of one of the richest families in the western world then a more agreeable way of life might be open to him in some other place. Even if Joyce's wife denied him a divorce . . .

'Of course, things may change now Mr O'Hara's gone.' Small offered this gratuitous comment without emphasis.

'You mean in terms of the pious observance of the Catholic view on matrimony?'

'Something like that, sir, yes. As far as I could see, it was Mr O'Hara who set the pace – for the people at the top, anyway.'

'Because he controlled the purse-strings. But won't his brother . . . ?'

'From what I can gather Mr Paul O'Hara won't be much concerned with keeping people on the strait and narrow – nor with the island either, except for what he can get out of it.'

So the Chief Minister, thought Treasure, might be said to have been presented with the penny and the bun through the sad demise of Joe O'Hara – additional power, and freedom from rules that constrained his way of life.

'You said Paul O'Hara knew his brother was sleeping at the cabin. He wasn't at the dinner last night?'

'No, sir, he wasn't. Arrived while it was on, came ashore and made himself at home in Buckingham House. He makes fairly regular trips here – uses that floating gin-palace to ship cigars to the States . . .'

'Which would make his cruises tax deductible,' Treasure put in knowingly.

Small nodded. 'I expect so. Anyway, he admitted he had a flaming row with his brother and that Mr Joe left for the cabin around midnight – probably in the cause of a quiet life.'

'You've seen Paul O'Hara?'

'Yes. I went straight to the house after I'd finished up

at the Falls. He's a cool customer. Made no bones about his relations with his brother, and didn't express any particular concern about what happened. You know, he didn't even want to see the body. The only thing that seemed to throw him was the decapitation.'

'He learnt about the death from you? But it must have been some hours after . . .'

'Not about the death, sir, no. A young kitchen maid, the only servant on duty and incidentally his alibi – ' Small glowered disapprovingly – 'she wakened him about nine o'clock and told him Mr Joe was dead, but for some reason hadn't mentioned the, er . . . the foul play – perhaps to spare his feelings.'

Treasure nodded. 'Understandable, perhaps. It's odd, though, the chap didn't ask how his brother came to kick the bucket.'

'He assumed it was a heart attack.'

'Assumed? Well, that was a thundering big assumption . . .'

'Not the way he put it, sir. Mr Joe had had heart trouble for years.'

'And you said O'Hara jibbed at the idea of a post-mortem.'

'Mm – though I can't imagine why he should think we could've avoided one.' Small picked up the telephone whose ring had punctuated his last remark. 'All right, I'll come out.' He replaced the receiver. 'Father Babington is here asking to see me.'

'One of the top people.' Treasure grimaced and stood up. 'I'll make myself scarce.'

CHAPTER XIV

Paul O'Hara surveyed the contents of his brother's desk. These, together with material he had removed from the wall safe, he had stacked in untidy piles on the desk top.

He had gleaned very little new information from his hardly authorized examination of Joe's private papers.

He was not his brother's legal executor. He had hoped to come upon a copy of Joe's will, but in this he was disappointed. He automatically became the owner of King Charles Industries Ltd., but he would need to wait upon Joe's lawyers and bankers on Grand Cayman to learn how the fool had arranged the dissipation of his private possessions – and what they amounted to in cash terms.

Paul was quite ready to challenge Joe's intentions if the private estate was substantial. He was certain his brother would have bequeathed him nothing – that everything would be made over to one or other of the KCI charitable trusts. Preventing even the smallest flow of more O'Hara capital into any of these wholly undeserving activities would give him satisfaction beyond the sum of the pecuniary gain.

In demanding and obtaining Joe's keys from that temporarily rattled policeman, Paul had confidently believed he had secured access to any amount of material that would throw at least a ridiculous and at best an unsavoury light on the character of the brother he did not one bit lament. In this, too, his expectations had been unrealized.

There were no private sets of account books, no diaries, no letters – nothing in the least incriminating or salacious. His hopes had been especially dashed in the last connection. He had long harboured the view that Joe's much promoted saintly persona was far too flawless to be true. Did the man really sublimate all his human desires in that endless pursuit of pious intentions? Could the character who had hatched the whole cigar caper have been so unspotted in relation to all other forms of conventional sin?

The cigar caper: curse that humbug of a priest for his misdirected loyalty. By all accounts he had roundly and publicly condemned Joe as a traitor – and two hours later mindlessly ordered the destruction of the source of continuing bounties – all on the unsupported premise that such wanton profligacy accorded with Joe's wishes.

Well, the premise had been almost unsupported: the irony was that the sanctimonious Babington had Joe wrongly cast as a traitor in the first place. At least the idiot had been dissuaded from consigning a three months' stock of cigars to the incinerator's unappreciative maw. Hell's teeth, that had been a close call – involving a best forgotten, undignified bit of crawling. At least the reward would compensate for the indignity; the cigars might be the last profitable shipment, but the satisfied customers would be paying cash on delivery – there would be no invoices from KCI this time.

O'Hara calculated the value of his personal benefit from this last machination – and made a note to be at the quayside personally to supervise the unloading of the train from the convent at two o'clock.

He was of a mind to quit the island as soon as the yacht was loaded, but prudence suggested he should remain until the results of the autopsy were available. His intention then was to have the yacht take him to Grand Cayman before the Captain sailed it back to Miami. He could spend the next day clearing the legal and financial business. He supposed he would need to return to KCI for Joe's funeral – even Paul O'Hara recognized this elemental obligation. In any case, his own lawyer would be flying down to meet him in the morning, and having him on hand in Rupertstown for the following week would be a justifiable expense.

The big deal with Dogwall could simmer on the back burner for a while – that's how the man himself had put it, and with scarcely disguised enthusiasm about the ultimate outcome. Dogwall was hooked, but with Joe's puppet, Mr High-and-Mighty Joyce, flexing his constitutional muscles there would have to be a hiatus – until ways were found to cut the Chief Minister down to size, as well as to expose the posturings of the ludicrous Rees. The Governor

appeared to have graduated from train-spotter to Lord
Protector in one short morning. O'Hara could only
suppose that the epidemic of arrogance was a measure of
how surely his brother had suppressed and inhibited the
ambitions of others – which proved there was some good
even in Joe.

Soberly he concluded that for the time being at least he
had to avoid giving Rees and Joyce grounds for invoking
the support of the British Government in opposition to his
plans. KCI being to all appearances a self-supporting
Crown Colony, Whitehall would be only too ready to
defend the status quo on the island. Once it became
evident that the economy was heading for bankruptcy,
then London would start playing a different tune. If
eventually the choice lay between mounting an expensive
aid programme or accepting American financial succour
available for the asking he had no doubt which course
would appeal most.

O'Hara needed to take his time – and happily he could
now afford to do so. It was always possible that in the
interim he could bring Babington back to a saner view on
the cigar business – possible but, he had to admit to himself, not exactly probable. As an alternative, selling the
cigar company to the Anglo-Australian interest would
upset nobody. He could scarcely prevent himself from
laughing aloud at the prospect of bringing off this particular coup. Damn it, they could put in their distillery too
if they wanted – it would all help the Paul O'Hara cash
flow and improve the value of King Charles Industries.

The new owner of Buckingham House stroked his beard
and passed his gaze over the contents and decorations of
the sombre library. The edifice in which the room was
contained was the part of the inheritance which he would
gladly have forsworn: perhaps he could sell it to an oil-
rich Arab or a social-climbing dentist. In any event, it
could hardly be said seriously to mar the fresh prospect
that stretched enticingly ahead.

O'Hara sighed; it was irritating that his sense of secure

contentment stopped short of immoderate proportions –
due only to the unfathomable action of a person unknown.
He wished hell fire on the meddling fool who had cut off
his brother's head.

Glen Dogwall, naked and muscles straining, shadow-
boxed before the full-length mirror in the guest-house
bathroom. He had made only rare and youthful appearances in the boxing ring. Being well past the age when he
could be required to do so again, apart from becoming a
keen spectator of the sport, he was the source of so many
fictitious tales concerning his exploits as a young pugilist
that he had come to believe them himself.

In his mind's eye he downed Mongo Joyce with a well-
timed blow to the head and danced back, rolling his heavy
shoulders at the mirror, while a mythical referee counted
out the completely out-classed and equally invisible
Chief Minister.

This part of the fantasy exhausted, Dogwall struck a
succession of poses to reconfirm his conviction that only
age and status denied him the opportunity to run for the
Mr Universe title. He then went into his Fred Astaire
dance routine, snapping his fingers to the rhythm of 'How
About You', and humming a version of the melody that
even Cole Porter might have found difficult to distinguish
from the British National Anthem. The choreography
attaching to this part of the exhibition limited the per-
former to backward and forward steps – the narcissistic
satisfaction ceased abruptly outside the limited confines of
what the mirror could reflect.

Dogwall's sense of self-admiration was now beginning
to peak and he was ready to go into his finale. Unfortunately this involved co-operation – not to mention
assistance – from his wife. He chasséed to the bathroom
door; she was still not back. The message from Government House that had greeted his return from seeing
O'Hara had simply indicated she had gone on a train ride.
He snorted his displeasure: the fact that his wife had

chosen an arguably less incongruous midday occupation than the one he had in mind for her did not enter his thoughts. He had not married the woman so that she could take unscheduled trips at times inconvenient to himself.

He stepped into the shower. In response to his turning the tap to full volume the rusty rose emitted a power-less sprinkle that scarcely bore comparison with the performance of a watering-can. He sat down on the floor of the little cubicle and pretended it was raining.

Paul O'Hara had jokingly suggested that he, Glen Dogwall the Third, had cut off his brother's head – and got away with it. He had given up hotly denying the accusation because the guy had quickly made it plain it was only a ghoulish joke: it had still been unnerving. More – Paul had blandly indicated that Joe's demise had been the most desirable of issues. Dogwall shook his head; that took some beating – the man's own brother and he was practically ordering imported champagne for the wake.

Well, Rachel would alibi him up to the eyebrows – as soon as he could find her and tell her exactly what to say. Joe O'Hara had got what was coming to him all right. The double-cross had been more than Dogwall could stomach. Paul had promised not to let out he had tipped him off the night before about the deal being a set-up – that was something else Rachel would need telling about. There was no point in the police figuring he had a motive: Paul had said as much in passing. Dogwall had not reacted at the time because he had had something else on his mind – sole ownership of King Charles Industries, no less.

He was sure it had been Paul's phone call to the Governor and Joyce that had fixed it. If they had been in the least bit ready to co-operate over the original Sunfun deal, O'Hara would never have gotten so furious and later confidentially offered to sell out what amounted to control of the whole damned island. True, his opening price had sounded steep – but that was before they got on to the idea of a discounted, part payment through Switzerland. Well, the Sunfun Hotel Corporation of America knew more than most outfits about how to avoid capital gains tax – you could almost say they were experts. O'Hara could be accommodated all right.

The soft island water trickled over Dogwall's flopped anatomy. He had stopped imagining himself in the ring or before the footlights. He smiled contentedly at the prospect of having everybody on this money-spinning little island working for him, including that smart-ass lawyer of a Chief Minister, Mongo Joyce – especially Mongo Joyce. And there was nothing the bastard could do about it – which also went for his buddy-boy Governor.

Altogether things looked pretty good to Glen Dogwall – since he was contemplating upon rather than taking cognizance of his creased-up, less than athletic trunk, now settled in slack repose. One thing he failed to figure was why Paul had confided the belief there would be no murder charge over his brother's death – when everybody knew the guy had his head cut off. It was not that he hoped Paul was wrong; on the contrary, if he was right then who was going to care about alibis anyway?

Mongo Joyce watched his secretary close the door as she left his office. She had not expected to be called to work today, but she had come in with a good grace. So had all the other people he had summoned to help deal with the situation. There was no doubt he commanded loyalty.

With this consoling thought in mind he stood up and walked to the window. The room was at the front of the combined KCI courthouse and government administrative building across the square from the police-station block.

The decorated, beflagged platform stood deserted, like the square itself. Even the intended good-humoured expression on the face of the King Charles statue seemed to have saddened – as though to point the thought that the platform it faced could easily do service as gallows or bandstand.

Eric Small had been right. The Chief Minister had wasted not a minute of the morning, and establishing witness to his whereabouts during the previous night had been first on the list of priorities. After leaving the Governor he had gone straight to his home. His wife had accepted her instructions without demur, question or show of emotion. He had telephoned Cynthia from the office. She had been no less co-operative – but she had needed to be persuaded that events had not created the perfect opportunity for ending moral pretentions. Her impatience had been assuaged by Joyce's stricture that authorship of the particular event he had in mind had yet to be established. She had agreed that a wife's testimony, if lacking in objectivity, was somehow more respectable than a mistress's – if only because it begged fewer additional questions.

What Joyce saw spread out before him in his mind's eye was not an empty square but the fulfilment of his ambition. He would now lead KCI forward to independence and ultimately to a status in the Caribbean that would put its importance far ahead of its size.

First would come the referendum: with Joe gone and Archie Rees pledging moral support, self-determination for KCI within the Commonwealth was a foregone conclusion. Once the people realized the profitable future that lay ahead there would be no cause for opposition. He, Mongo Joyce, would decide when it was time to create an opposition – a cosy one, just big enough to prove he was running a democracy. This was a low priority in the time-scale but it was as well not to forget its ultimate importance.

After independence, King Charles Industries Ltd. and all its subsidiary and associated companies would be nationalized – not confiscated, but taken into state ownership at a fair price with stage payments spread over five years. Cynthia Franks-Barrett would arrange to place three million dollars at the community's disposal, at nominal interest.

Joe O'Hara's insane decision to phase out the tobacco business would be immediately reversed. Personally Joyce had never been able to understand why Americans prized King Charles Elegantes so highly, but with a turnover of five million dollars a year he wanted to see the activity expanded. If the nuns were unwilling to co-operate he would soon recruit people who would – even if he had to bring them from Cuba or Jamaica.

The distillery project and the hydro-electric scheme were both critically important ventures. Joyce was not so ingenuous as to suppose that foreign capitalists would be queueing to invest in a heavily nationalized economy. Nevertheless, his plans very much included new partnership enterprises, and with the right kind of tax advantages and guarantees he was confident he could overcome initial diffidence. He was nothing if not confident.

The King is dead. Long live the . . . The Chief Minister's gaze re-focused on the statue in the square. He wondered again who it was had indulged in the so appropriate act of beheading Joe O'Hara – the already dead Joe O'Hara.

Sir Archibald and Lady Rees were taking a light luncheon at one end of the long table in the dining-room of Government House.

The Governor regarded a forkful of cold corn with distaste. He directed his gaze at his wife, an action that did nothing to induce a change of expression. 'I still think the arrangements for the Treasures –'

'Are perfectly adequate,' Lady Rees interrupted firmly. 'Molly,' she continued, pausing to emphasize and to savour the easy familiarity she had established with her celebrated guest, 'Molly doesn't care for food in the middle of the day. Actresses have to watch their figures even more carefully than the rest of us.' She helped herself to another piece of *quiche lorraine* without flinching. 'In any case, Debby's with her. Mark specifically asked to be excused.'

'He volunteered to help Small – seems he has some kind of connection with the police.'

Rees would have been a good deal more at ease if Treasure had been beside him sharing this dismal, cold collation. There was no call for the chap to be playing amateur detective. The position was obvious enough. Joe had died of a coronary – his third in as many years. The autopsy would show as much. Even Small had deduced the decapitation had been intended as symbolism – fitting the day and marking the end of a dynasty. It mattered very little who was responsible – which was as well, since no one was ever going to know. Gore could have been an unseen and unexpected witness, but the fellow must have been asleep at the time or else he would have raised the alarm earlier. The Governor wondered how long the Jamaicans would take to confirm the cause of death. The whole business would have been much better confined to KCI; doctors should know better than to get food poisoning. He frowned at what looked like half a fly in his salad.

Joyce had the right ideas. One had to move with the times. Joe O'Hara's paternalism had been a hundred years out of date. KCI could become a model independency within the Commonwealth. The Chief Minister was no republican: he showed a proper regard for the Crown – and respect for the Queen's representative. Together they could do great things. People had needed to be brought to a prompt understanding of the opportunity – shocked into it.

'I'm going to have my rest directly. Don't you want to finish that salad?' Lady Rees scooped up and consumed the remains; her husband watched with special interest. 'I'm nearly asleep already. If you must get up at unearthly hours I wish you'd do so without waking me.'

He had tried.

Peregrine Gore pushed down even harder on the driving

bar. 'We must be doing twenty at least.' He beamed at
the exhausted McLush who was see-sawing opposite with
less enthusiasm and waning effort.

For Peregrine the ride to freedom on the rail trolley car
was pure exhilaration. He had even been excused the
embarrassment of exposing his presence – not to mention a
good deal too much of his person – to a strange nun. If
he could maintain the speed of the little vehicle into the
engine yard at Rupertstown and sprint the short distance
to the police-station in the square he was certain his
problems would be over.

McLush was less ebullient. The way things were
ordered, he had long since come to consider himself a
second-rate journalist and a third-rate spy. He was now
resigned to accepting fourth-rate status as a burglar:
finding oneself imprisoned in premises one had entered to
pillage hardly justified a higher rating. It was also now
apparent that his nocturnal and clandestine expedition to
an area of the island close to Devil's Falls conferred
first-rate standing as a murder suspect. The fact that his
incarceration in the cigar factory had gone unwitnessed –
at least up to the moment of release – promised to deepen
his plight in the last connection. It was no solace that he
had added to his experience the knowledge that while
gravity aided – even accelerated – ingress effected by way
of vertical ventilation shafts, it definitely inhibited egress
by the same route.

Gore and McLush had been afforded ample opportunity
to exchange news and views on current affairs while
sheltering in the sugar cane. It would be an overstatement to record that the journalist had been at first disposed
to offer so expansive an account of events as his companion in adversity.

It was not until Peregrine had disclosed the death of
Joe O'Hara – and its apparent cause – that McLush had
deduced an extra vulnerability in his own position.
Thereafter he had taken pains not only to provide a
plausible explanation for his presence at the convent but

also to impress that he had inadvertently imprisoned himself there since one o'clock in the morning.

It emerged that it had been McLush who had cut the hole in the fence – the one quickly adapted by the flower-eating pig for watering expeditions to the river between courses. The secrecy surrounding the whole cigar-making process had been offered as reason enough for a thrusting, investigative journalist to seek enlightenment by methods admittedly illegal – but trespass was a different class of crime to murder. He had not troubled to mention that if the contents of the plastic bag in his pocket proved to be as metaphorically explosive as he suspected, then his promotion from ignorable hack to Pulitzer Prize ranking might yet be assured.

Borrowing the rail car had proved to be the easiest of devices adapted by either of its present elevated occupants when compared to earlier recourses – that they had stolen it would be too strong an admission taking into account the conspicuous appearance of the vehicle and the unlikelihood of its usage passing unnoticed for very long. Simply, the pair had taken advantage of Sister He'ena's temporary absence from the scene – she had done a controlled bolt into the factory – to race over the open ground, mount the conveyance, and propel it through the gates.

That the nuns were expecting visitors – either by rail or via the unmade road that skirted the railway – had been obvious since the gates were first unlocked. The hazard of meeting an oncoming train had thus been Peregrine's prime concern from the start of the journey. Since it was he who had been, as it were, travelling backwards, he had cautioned the bespectacled McLush accordingly. He had not thought about the probable incidence of points on what was evidently a branch line, an omission which had already led to one derailment – where the convent line joined KCI's main track. The spill had not been a catastrophy, but now that the ill-assorted pair were on their way again it was Peregrine who had taken up the rear operating position. They had stopped short at the points that served up-coming trains bound for Gull Rock, but these – as expected – had been set in their favour.

'From a distance,' the young Englishman gasped, 'we must look like a couple of Orientals caught up in one of these bowing and scraping routines.' McLush appeared not to appreciate the analogy. 'Do trains ever go to Gull Rock?' Peregrine continued good-humouredly.

'No.' McLush had not overcome his irritation at having failed to prevent the derailment; he was supposed to be something of an authority on railways – especially this one.

'But the line's still usable?'

Why couldn't the fellow concentrate on the job? 'Only just,' McLush replied grudgingly. 'The viaduct from the mainland's rotting, and the pier's not sound.'

'There's a pier? Out to sea, you mean?'

'That's where they usually go. This one was used to berth small vessels . . .'

'And to load them by rail?'

Whatever further intelligence McLush was ready to vouchsafe he had no time to utter.

'Hand brake on!' Peregrine shouted like a well-drilled gunner. 'Steam train approaching – with a wonky whistle by the sound of it.'

Samuel Breese Morse had enjoyed better tribute than that to his inventiveness.

CHAPTER XV

Treasure surveyed the statue of Charles the First with favour – and the group of young boys using its plinth for football practice with a matching degree of disapproval. The effigy of the martyred King had a quiet dignity about it – and though slender and lonely, it dominated the square. The figure looked vital – in contrast to the Empire-studding memorials to Queen Victoria which, no matter how solid the stone, seemed always to invest that monarch with the appearance of a massive, wilting blancmange: there was also the invariable suggestion that the old Queen had been immortalized at the very moment of smelling something obnoxious.

The banker ambled across the square in the direction of the Royal Crown Hotel whose Colonial frontage occupied most of the eastern side. Chief Inspector Small had promised to meet him in the colonnade bar at one o'clock; it was already a few minutes past the hour but Treasure was first to arrive. He seated himself in a raffia chair at one of the pavement tables and noted that he was the sole customer.

In the twenty minutes that had elapsed since he had left the police-station Treasure had turned out of the town square on to the wide, cobbled quay. He had first inspected the handsome, lonely motor yacht moored at the centre of the long, main jetty. This had prompted him to wonder why the resourceful O'Hara had not suggested developing the underused harbour as a marina for ocean-going yachts. By all accounts such complexes were profitable and, in view of the island's history, attracted a more desirable class of affluent caller than the self-confessed pirates of yesteryear – even if in some cases personal acquaintance suggested the distinction might be blurred.

Treasure had next followed the railway track that served the quayside a hundred yards or so westwards to the engine shed and past this to the bridge that constituted the end of town. The view from there, back across the town and harbour, had been a pleasing one – the buildings neat, the rows of small fishing-boats in the shore end lee of the eastern mole picturesque, the island's statelier edifices behind – the Baroque church, the Governor's residence, even the incongruous Buckingham House further up the hill – lending an air of seasoned solidity to the scene.

Apart from a seaman washing paintwork on the yacht there had been no visible human activity. Treasure recalled his wife's conjecture that the population had still been breakfasting at nine-thirty – an indulgence that had perhaps been strung out to an hour when it could respectably be replaced by the taking of lunch.

He had threaded his way back to the square along a narrow, curving street of shuttered shops below and a curious mixture of bunting and drying washing hanging above; if the men of Rupertstown were resigned – in deference to Joe O'Hara – to spending the day at home, their womenfolk were clearly less inclined to inactivity.

The blare of record-players and radios thudding in upstairs rooms, the resonance through open windows baffled by the houses opposite – a characteristic of mean streets on hot days – at least witnessed the existence of a population. But the sailor and the children playing in the square had been the only human beings Treasure had actually observed at close quarters. He looked around for a waiter only to be confronted by an evidently agitated Mr Brown who had made a sudden appearance from the interior of the hotel.

The new arrival mopped his wig-fringed brow with an orange face-flannel. He regarded this object with a mixture of embarrassment and displeasure. 'Packed in a hurry, you see, forgot my hankies. I'm so sorry.'

Treasure took the awkward apology more as evidence of acute unease than as a profession of conscious regret. 'You must allow me to lend you a few until the shops open,' he offered, but purely as earnest of good intention; he did not care to lend handkerchiefs or combs. 'Shall you be staying long?'

Brown cast about him with what his companion considered an unusually wide sweep of the head for anyone not engaged in directing traffic. It was then that Treasure remembered the artificial eye.

'Do sit down,' said the banker, having simultaneously recalled the artificial leg. 'Can I get you a drink?'

Brown sank into a chair. 'Most kind of you, sir . . . er, Mr Treasure. Just the one might . . . that is . . . um . . . dear me – ' he interjected a sigh – 'I really must be giving the worst sort of impression. You see, I believe there may have been another fatality.' This last statement came out with a rush.

'You mean you know someone else has pegged out – or you just think so?'

Brown shook his head vigorously from side to side. 'Only an assumption on my part – but if the murder of Mr O'Hara was to do with the cigar company I have every reason to fear for the safety of the gentleman I'm here to see.'

'Well, it's far from certain O'Hara was murdered, Mr Brown. His body was mutilated but the police think that happened after death. It's conceivable he died from natural causes. They're doing an autopsy to find out.' Treasure smiled reassuringly. 'Who is it you're concerned about?'

'A Mr Angus McLush . . .'

'The writer,' Treasure nodded. 'He's missing, but not, I think, believed killed,' he added lightly. 'Tell me, what's your interest in the cigar company – or is it a secret?'

Brown appeared to hesitate. 'Oh dear, this really is very awkward.' He ran his tongue over his lips. 'I work for a bank, Mr Treasure.'

'So do I.'

'I know that, sir, but I really am very small fry in comparison . . . that is, well even without comparison.' Brown gave a short cough. 'I look after the interests of a Swiss banking group in the Caribbean.'

'How very agreeable.'

'Er . . . yes, and as you might suppose, not at all arduous. I was lucky to secure the post some years ago – I was in London then, though I'd had a good deal of experience out here with a Canadian bank. But that's of no consequence. My employers are Grifer, Lerc of Zürich.'

'Well, I never. And how's Pierre Lerc?'

'He's the President.'

Treasure chuckled. 'I know, and a very old friend. Charming chap.'

'I'm sure, though I fear I've never had the pleasure.'
Brown hesitated again, but his expression changed from
one of uncertainty into something approaching determination. 'This is in confidence, Mr Treasure, but in the
circumstances I'm sure . . .'

'I shall observe your confidence. But shall we order that
drink? Lager or something stronger?' A white-coated
waiter had at last appeared and was eyeing the two more
out of curiosity than by way of anticipating their need for
service. Brown nodded. 'Two Carlsbergs, please.' The
waiter retreated without comment or, as Treasure
divined from experience in more sophisticated premises,
any commitment as to brand.

'The bank has a customer, Mr Treasure,' Brown was
continuing, 'to whom we have been making regular and
substantial advances against earnings from the King
Charles Tobacco Company.'

'But without security?'

'Um, in a sense, yes. It's a private company, of course,
and its component parts . . .'

'Amount to an operation rather than a tangible
organization, or a negotiable asset.'

'Precisely. The customer is Grade A with the bank,
however, and funds do materialize on due dates.'

'But the bank often has a largish balance at risk.'

Brown nodded agreement. 'Which is why we, as it were,
keep an eye on the island in general and the tobacco
company in particular. Some time ago we made an
arrangement with Mr McLush to . . .'

'To keep you posted?'

The face flannel appeared again and was used to mop
the glistening brow. 'The arrangement was on a very
confidential basis for fear of offending susceptibilities. Mr
McLush was not . . . er, is not aware the bank is retaining
his services.'

Treasure affected mild surprise. 'Then who . . . ?'

'He was led to suppose – indeed, he virtually led himself
to suppose he was in the pay of some national intelligence

service.' There was an embarrassed pause before Brown continued. 'I fear it was I who encouraged this . . . this, er, harmless subterfuge.'

'In case he was caught poking his nose into other people's affairs and was obliged to offer an explanation?'

'Exactly, Mr Treasure.' Brown nodded eagerly. 'I should add that Zürich is not privy to . . . er . . .'

'To McLush's belief he's a spy.' Treasure chuckled. 'He doesn't sell vacuum-cleaners as a cover, does he?'

The allusion was lost on Brown. 'No, he's a journalist by profession,' he answered seriously. 'It was in that capacity that yesterday he discovered through an informant that the tobacco company was to be sold for a sum a lot lower than the price we'd been led to believe it was worth. I transmitted this information to Switzerland and was immediately instructed to order Mr McLush to . . . er . . . to press some further enquiry.'

'Of what nature? I mean, what did you tell him to do?'

Brown sighed. 'To obtain samples of the cigars currently being produced.'

Treasure was all too aware of the difficulties that might attend such a task. 'Did you instruct him to break into the factory? It's part of a convent.'

'That I left to his discretion,' Brown answered hurriedly. 'In any event, I told him that another agent –' he coughed nervously – 'that's me of course, would be here this morning to confer. I took the first flight from Grand Cayman to Montego Bay. I was not aware there was no morning flight from there to King Charles. You know the rest.'

'But there's no sign of McLush. Frankly, I should say it's a little early to imagine he's . . .' Treasure allowed his voice to tail off. The waiter had returned with glasses and two cans of Red Stripe beer; it was some consolation to note that the cans were frosted.

When the two men were alone again it was Treasure who re-opened the conversation. 'I assume you're not able to reveal the name of the bank's customer.'

'The point is academic, Mr Treasure. I don't know it.'

Treasure nodded, and mentally calculated the time of day in Zürich. He imagined he could himself put a name to the man whose expenditure exceeded his income from the King Charles Tobacco Company – but it would be nice to have the point confirmed. It would have been ingenuous to suppose that such information was available for the asking, even between friends, but if the directors of Grifer, Lerc were so anxious to obtain up-to-date intelligence on the status of the cigar company Treasure was perhaps in a better position to supply it than McLush, and since one good turn deserved another . . .

The little procession that entered the square at the corner furthest from where the two men were seated had – at that distance – the appearance of a refugee band. At the head was Debby Rees – resolute, but advancing at the limp. Behind her, in line abreast, came Molly Treasure, Peregrine and Mrs Dogwall. The group then reverted to single file, McLush in black, followed by Luke Murphy in a boiler suit and armed with a monkey-wrench.

Treasure noted with some satisfaction that his wife was the only member of the party whose appearance and demeanour were normal beyond remark. All the others in some way evidenced either affliction, extreme apprehension, or an eccentricity of dress that would have produced very loud remarks – not to say cat-calls – in many built-up areas.

The woman flanking Peregrine to his right – Treasure could only guess at the identity of Small's bobby-dazzler – wore a flimsy, sleeveless yellow jacket that stopped short some inches above her naval. This relatively decorous attire served to emphasize the near naked state of the shapely anatomy below. Apart from her high-heeled shoes Mrs Dogwall's only other defence from vulgar gaze were some brief white panties of a style that would never have been allowed daylight exhibition on the beach at Frinton.

But if Mrs Dogwall quickly earned the admiring

whistles of the erstwhile footballers in the square – a sequence that seemed to cause her no disquiet – it was Peregrine who produced the jeers; Peregrine Gore in a mini-length pleated yellow skirt worn over pale white skin and matching bare feet.

It was only seconds after the human convoy entered the square from the west that the motorized contingent of police tore in from the east. Two Land-Rovers skidded to a halt in front of the police-station and eight armed officers disgorged at the double.

'Stay where you are.' It was Debby who issued the order in a tone that did justice to a Governor's daughter. The ranks behind her closed perceptibly around Peregrine. The policemen halted, irresolute.

Father Babington chose this moment to make his departure from the police-station. Treasure and Brown were already hurrying across the square.

'Arrest that man – he's a spy. I have recorded proof.' McLush had detached himself from the group and was advancing upon Brown, arm pointed in accusation.

'He's nothing of the sort, Mr McLush, and I advise you to keep silent.' Treasure had taken a stance on the unclaimed ground between the police and the rescue party.

'Now, sergeant,' he addressed the leading officer, 'some of these ladies and gentlemen are going in to see Chief Inspector Small. Kindly clear the way. Miss Rees – ' he turned to Debby – 'perhaps you'd lead in Mr McLush and Mr Gore. Good afternoon, Peregrine.'

The sergeant glanced at Father Babington, who nodded in support of the banker's instructions: the summary execution of Peregrine Gore had been avoided once again.

Debby limped up the station steps followed by the two men – and by Mrs Dogwall who kept close to Peregrine's side; her role as protector might be concluded but she needed to retrieve her skirt.

'I think yellow suits him, don't you?' Molly Treasure had moved to her husband's side. 'Darling, you were marvellous – and so were the others. Hello, Mr Brown, enjoying your holiday?' She smiled benignly at the recipient of this inapposite enquiry. 'Peregrine and his friend positively ran into us riding on a trolley – so inventive. Mr Murphy here hitched them up, and here we are.'

Treasure held out his hand to Luke Murphy. 'How d'you do. Thank you for guarding the party. D'you know, at first sight in that boiler suit, I thought you were the Governor.'

The black man smiled. 'Difference is, sah, on me de dirt don't show.'

CHAPTER XVI

It was an hour since the confrontation in the square. Treasure returned to the Chief Inspector's office after completing his telephone call in another room.

'You get through all right?'

'Mm. Your operator's extremely efficient.' Treasure settled himself in a chair.

Small appreciated the compliment and privately wished it could be applied to the general functioning of the KCI police force. 'Was Babington right?'

'He was right to tell you Joe O'Hara thought he was being blackmailed by McLush – but the late O'Hara was wrong. McLush receives a small quarterly retainer from the bank. He has no account there – numbered or otherwise. Joe probably got to know McLush was receiving cheques from Grifer, Lerc . . .'

Small nodded. 'That's simple. He was President of the KCI Bank.'

'So he put two and two together. If O'Hara was making blackmail payments to a Grifer, Lerc account it would have been easy to assume McLush was the villain. He wasn't.'

'Who was?'

'Pierre Lerc isn't telling, I'm afraid – not for the

moment anyway, and certainly not on an open telephone line. It's understandable. The blackmail allegation is, after all, second-hand. I made the mistake of volunteering we thought Joe had been murdered – a point that considerably strengthened Pierre's sense of integrity. In fairness, I'd have reacted in the same way.'

'But he did confirm it isn't McLush who's been getting these er . . . these alleged substantial payments from Joe O'Hara.'

'Definitely. Of course, you could say he's protecting an employee . . .'

'But the explanation and the misunderstanding – they're logical enough.' Small frowned. 'Which leaves us guessing.'

'True, but if O'Hara was being blackmailed by someone else who benefited from the cigar business, we're looking at a pretty small field.' Treasure helped himself to a banana from the plate on Small's desk. The two had agreed to go without a proper lunch. 'Incidentally, I'd guess friend Brown is in for a wigging for panicking and disclosing all – or all he knew. Poor chap.' But the speaker did not appear unduly concerned.

'And if the cigar company is just a front for drug trafficking as McLush says?'

'He's not going to say it to anyone else?' Treasure countered quickly.

'Not a chance, sir. He's scared stiff.' Small glanced at the plastic bag sitting in the centre of his blotting-pad. 'That's marijuana all right, and very high quality too – ganga they call it out here. We've only McLush's word on where he got it, of course.'

'And you've cautioned him he could be charged with illegal possession.'

Small shrugged his shoulders. 'He didn't disclose it voluntarily. We found it when we searched him after he'd admitted breaking and entering the convent. What's really got him worried is the chance he'll be arrested on suspicion of murder.'

'Out all night, no alibi, close to the scene of the crime. By the way, thank you again for letting Gore leave.'

The Chief Inspector smiled before continuing. 'As far as I can ascertain, practically everybody at that dinner-party is ready to confirm that McLush and Mr O'Hara were at daggers drawn.'

'In fairness – according to Gore anyway – it was Joe O'Hara who had his knife into McLush, not the other way round.'

'True, and Father Babington's given us the reason.' Small paused. 'I had to shut up McLush, sir – for the time being anyway. This ganga business is dynamite. The implications . . .'

'Could suggest that everyone in authority on this pious little island is potentially a partner in the smoothest drug racket ever devised.' Treasure gave a chuckle.

KCI's temporary Police Chief was not moved to mirth. 'It's very serious, Mr Treasure.'

'I know, Chief Inspector.' The banker suppressed a further chuckle. 'But at least you're not implicated.'

Small sighed. 'Which may put me in a minority of one.'

'Not quite. You've got me. But I see what you mean. If the thing's organized on the scale McLush suggests, you can't even be sure your policemen aren't involved – and the Customs and Excise people next door.' Treasure paused. 'But hang on. McLush claims to be a professional ferret. He's lived here for years and it's taken him till today to discover a wholesale drug racket.'

'Or so he says when faced with a possible murder charge.'

'You've got a point there. I still think what evidence we've got could suggest the involvement of a very few people – most of them in a closed order of nuns.'

'Both the O'Haras have to be implicated, plus Father Babington. And what about the Chief Minister – even the Governor? This is a *very* small island, sir.'

Treasure marvelled that the policeman had not uncharitably decided to include Lady Rees. He stood up and walked to the window. 'I agree about the O'Haras, and obviously Babington. But it could stop right there. The nuns could have been growing the stuff under orders from Babington – same as they'd grow cauliflowers if he asked them to.'

'Oh?' Small vented his disbelief.

'No, I'm serious. Would they know they were in to some criminal activity? Marijuana's a soft drug anyway, and from what you tell me growing a bit in the garden's common enough in the West Indies.'

'It's still illegal and it's mostly leaf and stalk stuff. This is high quality material – more what you'd expect in a Thai stick.'

'A what?'

'Asian hashish – they get the resin from the flower of the female plant and wrap it round six-inch sticks. Very strong in THC it is – that's the active ingredient, tetra something or other. THC for short.' In answer to Treasure's surprised look Small added, 'I did a course in it last year.'

'Good for you. Anyway, back to basics. KCI ganga is high quality stuff, for export only, discounting consumption by stray pigs whose reactions confirm the power of the product. It's grown by the vicar for the local squire . . . Oh, and distributed in America by the squire's brother who happens to be in the smokes business. Now who else has to know? Customs people?'

Small shook his head. 'Not necessarily. They don't look at much that comes in, and they're certainly not bothered about what goes out.'

'And they can't see the stuff growing because no one gets into the convent. You don't see it from the air either because there's no overflying on that side of the island – to protect the birds. All clever stuff – arranged, no doubt, by Joe O'Hara.'

'I expect so. There's engine-drivers of course – the blokes who take the tobacco into the convent.'

'And who're probably made to stand by their engines

while the nuns unload the stuff. Gore says all you'd see from the convent building is a wall of sugar cane. No, I reckon that bit's fool-proof.' Treasure turned inwards from the window. 'It could be there are only three men in the know.'

'Plus whoever was blackmailing Mr O'Hara.'

'Unless . . .' Treasure paused, then squared his shoulders. 'What about Mongo Joyce – he must benefit through the tobacco company, but only indirectly on the face of it. You say he refused to sanction a search warrant?'

'Unless Father Babington approved.'

'That's rich. Tell me again exactly what Babington said when you had him back.'

'He said he had no knowledge of the existence of ganga at the convent – he said it twice.'

'And you'll be allowed into the convent at three o'clock without a warrant?'

Small nodded and glanced at his watch. 'An hour from now – any earlier would have interfered with devotions apparently.'

'You wouldn't think of going over Joyce's head to the Governor?'

'I'd rather not, sir.'

'I see what you mean. What a very sensitive situation. Joyce may be co-operating with Babington for purely political reasons – I mean nothing to do with the ganga, though that's the kindest possible interpretation in the circumstances. If you went to see Rees and he supported the other two there'd be a nasty cloud of suspicion over his head if a scandal breaks. Hm. Better wait for three o'clock, I think. Want me to come with you?'

'Very much, sir.' The Chief Inspector looked thoughtful. 'How d'you suppose they're getting the ganga into the USA? I mean, the Customs people there aren't sleepy.'

'That's the beauty of the whole business. My guess is they're not shipping marijuana. They're shipping cigars laced with marijuana under a special quota licence from the US Government!' Treasure dropped back into a chair.

'You see, the Americans regard the whole trade as something between a joke and an act of charity. I don't imagine shipments of KCI Elegantes get a second glance.' He nodded knowingly. 'This explains the whole unbelievable business.'

'How do you mean?'

'Chief Inspector, I've been invited to buy a highly-profitable operation at a knock-down price, with strings, it's true, but we're getting the cigar company for peanuts. The customers – that small and very select band of customers – have been paying close on ten dollars each for those cigars. Well, I wouldn't have paid a dollar for the ones I've sampled. So what's the explanation? According to Peregrine Gore, his late friend Mr Joe O'Hara had doubts about the survival of the KCI cigar trade. And how! For more than a decade Joe was making a very nice turn-out of very inferior cigars with a very special, home-grown additive.'

'Then along comes a blackmailer . . .'

'Precisely. Joe recognizes the game's up so there's to be a big switch into distilling or tourism with the apparently prosperous cigar company as the buyer bait. Incidentally, no one could have complained afterwards about the price of the tobacco company. Without the marijuana – sorry, ganga filling future profits would probably just about justify what Joe was asking.'

It was Small's turn to speculate. 'I understand there're about five hundred customers in the States. Would you say the blackmailer is likely one of them?'

Treasure shook his head. 'Possible, but if you think about it, not likely. You started out this morning looking for a murderer here on the island. Now you're interested in a blackmailer as well. Two crimes – two criminals? Or two crimes – one criminal? Right now I'd vote the second way. It complicates the motive, of course. Blackmailers don't normally polish off their victims . . .'

'Unless they're due for exposure or stand to gain more in the long run. Could I cadge another fill of that baccy,

Mr Treasure?'

'Please do. I think we could profitably spend the next half-hour smoking out our four hot prospects.'

'I make it six,' the Chief Inspector observed quietly as he proceeded to fill his pipe. 'That is if anyone's told me any fibs today. And I'm beginning to think they have.'

Molly Treasure had promised her husband she would not let Peregrine out of her sight. Since both Debby and Mrs Dogwall seemed obsessively keen to follow the same purpose Molly had no misgiving about leaving her charge in their care while she strolled in the garden of Government House. In any case, while she could not actually see the three of them, the noise of laughter and splashing from the guest-house pool was indication enough that Peregrine was safely occupied.

The short step-ladder and the secateurs Molly had found abandoned. She had temporarily borrowed both to aid in the execution of a minor piece of praedial larceny, namely the appropriation of some wild orchids that hung enticingly but just out of reach from a branch of a dogwood tree.

'Can I help, ma'am?'

Assistance was as unnecessary as the fact of being observed was irritating: nevertheless Molly gave the girl a warm smile. 'You can hold these clippers while I climb down. Sarah, isn't it?'

'Yes, ma'am.' The girl's face lit up. 'Please, ma'am, you're famous, aren't you? I seen you in de movies. Twice.'

'So you know I don't steal flowers for a living. Isn't that just beautiful?' Molly stepped down on to terra firma, and held up the spray of delicate blooms.

'Shall I be takin' back de ladder, ma'am?'

'Certainly not, Sarah. I'm sure you have better things to do in your free time. Isn't it a holiday?'

'It was supposed to be, ma'am, but Uncle Joe . . .'

'Of course, it's very sad. Did you know Mr O'Hara?'

The conventional enquiry produced an entirely un-expected reaction. Sarah burst into tears. Still clutching the secateurs, she dropped on her knees, her body con-vulsing with each heavy sob.

Molly sat down on the grass beside the girl. 'Sarah, I'm so sorry. I didn't mean to distress you.'

The tear-stained face was raised. 'Oh ma'am, someone gotta help me. Me got terrible trouble.'

Molly was a voluntary social counsellor in Chelsea. The situation was one she sensed as familiar enough; it was best to come to the point. 'Are you pregnant, Sarah?' she asked gently.

For once the lesson of experience was confounded. Nothing would have comforted Sarah more than to be able to answer that she was carrying the seed of the O'Haras. As it was, the question only served to deepen her despondency. She wept some more without replying.

Molly felt her fears confirmed. 'D'you want to tell me about it, Sarah? Here, take my hanky.' Unlike her fas-tidious husband, she matched the offer with action.

Sarah blew her nose. 'I was on de way to tellin' de Governor – it's him me should be tellin'. But me's scared, ma'am.'

The Governor indeed; the dirty old man – was Molly's outraged reaction: no wonder the child was in such a state. 'The Governor is the father, Sarah? Are you sure, now?'

The girl looked up again in blank surprise. 'No, ma'am, you don' understan' – it's not to do wid de Governor. It's de murder. I seen de murderer dis mornin' up at de lodge.'

CHAPTER XVII

Sister Helena was serene and composed – unlike the two men seated on the other side of her desk, both of whom sensed they were being outwitted. The nun's disarmingly contemplative gaze rested on neither of her visitors; it was fixed somewhere in the middle distance, although it suggested her thoughts were far away from her mundane surroundings.

In fact, Sister Helena was thinking how empty and ordered the little factory appeared after all the furious activity in the morning and the early afternoon. She also wondered – without apprehension – which way the questioning would now turn. Perhaps it would be as well to break the silence.

'Now is there any other mortal thing you'd like to be knowing, Chief Inspector?' The accent and the idiom bore a discernible and incongruous touch of the Irish – a legacy of five formative training years in County Cork, undissipated by over-indulgence in frivolous conversation in the ensuing quarter-century. 'I'm sure Reverend Mother won't want Mr McLush to be prosecuted – provided he doesn't practise such foolishness again.'

Small did his best not to show the exasperation he felt with this dissembling. He had practised the same self-control during the inspection of the recently ploughed lanes between the sugar canes as well as on the comprehensive tour of the cigar factory. The nun had studiously avoided recognizing that his visit with Treasure had been prompted by anything other than the burglary – an event that no one at the convent had seen fit to report in the first place.

The policeman looked sternly at the wilted *Cannabis sativa* bud and stem clasped in his left hand. It suggested the remains rather than the beginnings of a posy; but it was evidence – and there was plenty more in the turned-over earth outside.

'Very charitable of you, I'm sure, Sister.' The sarcasm in the tone was hardly disguised. Small was about to play his trump card. He produced a small plastic bag from his pocket. 'Of course, there's still the matter of the stolen property which, no doubt, you'll want returned.'

Sister Helena gazed at the bag: her cherubic, brown

countenance registered mystification. 'And what would that be, Chief Inspector?'

'That would be . . . that *is* a quantity of marijuana, Sister, which McLush alleges he stole from these premises.'

'Is it now? And that's what he alleges?' Sister Helena gave every indication that she was grateful for the enlightenment. 'And you're taking his word for it.' She shook her head sadly.

'Are you suggesting he didn't get it from here?'

'Not at all, Chief Inspector. Did you hear me make such a suggestion, Mr Treasure?'

'Certainly not, Sister,' said Treasure, with more conviction than he had intended. 'I gather McLush is quite insistent, though. He says there were trays of it in that storeroom where he came down the ventilator.'

'The empty one – with the strong smell of ammonia,' added Chief Inspector Small with extra emphasis.

'Ah, that was the infestation. You never saw so many creepy-crawlies. Came right in through the broken shaft, they did.' Sister Helena smiled at the two men in turn. 'A good scrub through with ammonia did the trick. We had to burn the stores – riddled they were with the dreadful creatures.'

'What did you have stored there, Sister?' Small was still holding his drooping bud.

'Ah, now that's difficult to say exactly, Chief Inspector. A bit of this, and a bit of that.' Sister Helena put her hands together in a prayerful gesture. 'Let me see now. There would have been dried herbs from the garden – oh, and seeds of all descriptions. I shouldn't allow it but Sister Geraldine – she was in charge of our garden – she used to say the atmosphere's just right for such things in here.'

'Used to say?'

'She passed away the week before last at the grand age of eighty-three – may she rest in peace.' Sister Helena made the sign of the Cross. Treasure, following the instinct of a High Anglican, did the same thing.

Small gave an embarrassed cough and tapped his chest. 'And only Sister Geraldine would have known what was in the storeroom, of course.' It was not so much a question as a statement. 'Are you saying, Sister, that this quantity of dried ganga couldn't have come from there?'

'Sister Geraldine was a great one for herbal remedies, Chief Inspector. She could work miracles.'

Since the late lamented did not immediately arrange to have Sister Helena struck by lightning, Treasure privately concluded the lady might also have been endowed with a broad mind and a strong sense of humour.

'Now it could be,' the nun continued earnestly, 'that Mr McLush happened upon some small quantity . . .'

'Of marijuana that Sister Geraldine had grown for medicinal purposes.' Small completed the statement with resignation in every syllable. 'All right, Sister, but was she also growing twenty acres of the stuff outside between the sugar canes? What I'm holding is a bud of *Cannabis sativa*.' He placed the limp specimen on the desk.

'Is that what it is now – well, you live and learn. To us it's the most pernicious weed in the place – would you believe?' Small gave not the slightest indication that he was anything other than a total disbeliever. 'We were ploughing it in only today as you could see. *Cannabis sativa*. I must make a note of that.' Sister Helena grasped a pencil and began to scribble. 'That would be double "n", I expect. Sister Geraldine was never able to find a weed-killer that would keep it down.' She looked up from her writing. 'Now is there anything else? With the terrible tragedy of Mr O'Hara you must have enough to do without chasing burglars.'

'Sister Helena –' it was Treasure who spoke – 'have you been putting ganga in the cigars?'

The hands returned to the prayerful position. 'Do you know, Mr Treasure, while we've been talking the thought has come to me that that's entirely possible.' The two men glanced at each other. Small produced a notebook. 'You see, we are always experimenting, with aromatics, you understand – ingredients that might make the cigars more popular.'

'From Sister Geraldine's bumper storeroom?' Treasure put in quietly.

'That's entirely right, Mr Treasure. And now you both have me worried that by chance . . .'

'You've been trafficking in drugs.' Small's tone was stern and sonorous.

'Ah, now that's a strong statement, Chief Inspector, and one you'd need to be proving, wouldn't you say?'

There was a pause. Small put his notebook away, made as though to retrieve his precious specimen, thought better of it, and stood up. 'Sister Helena, fifty shipping cases of cigars arrived in Rupertstown earlier this afternoon for loading. That's five thousand boxes of twenty-five cigars if my arithmetic's right.'

'That's absolutely right, Chief Inspector, and it's why we've not a cigar in the place here to offer you.'

Small continued. 'I have to tell you that Mr Broom of the Customs and Excise has seized the cargo for examination, and that I shall be receiving his report when we return to the town.'

'Well then, I mustn't delay you. With one thing and another you really have your hands full.' Sister Helena positively beamed at her two visitors as she showed them to the door. 'Reverend Mother will be all the more grateful when I tell her how you put yourself out –' she paused – 'investigating our little burglary.'

Mark and Molly Treasure, wearing swimming clothes, turned and retraced their steps along the unspoiled, palm-fringed beach. Treasure judged they had walked a mile around the headland – and further from the guest-house where they had earlier taken tea with Debby, Peregrine and the Dogwalls.

'The girl must have been mistaken. Small said it was still quite dark at five-thirty this morning.'

'But she saw someone,' Molly insisted, 'and if it wasn't Luke Murphy . . .'

Treasure interrupted, 'Well, it wasn't Luke Murphy. One mightn't accept the word of the three diesel engine-drivers – I mean he could have squared them – but if Archie Rees says the chap was in the railway yard from five to nearly six o'clock, you can't do much better than have the ruddy Governor as an alibi.'

'But the Governor wasn't there himself the whole time. You said . . .'

'He was playing trains some of the time. There was a panic on early because the precious *Sir Dafydd* was being temperamental. Rees took it on a test run by himself, and then drove the first train up. The point is, Murphy was there when he left and when he came back.'

'And there wouldn't have been time for him to nip up to this waterfall place, do for Joe O'Hara and . . . ?'

'Certainly not – it's miles. And anyway he still has other witnesses.' Treasure stopped to watch the gyrations of some diminutive fish. The shoal darted from the shallows seawards when Molly stepped into the water to join him for a closer look. 'Anyway, Small's playing it very close. As yet, nobody, including the Governor and the Chief Minister, knows about the autopsy result – nor about Sarah's awful experience,' he finished lightly.

'Well, it couldn't have been very funny for her, poor child.'

'No, of course not. You did the right thing, darling – in bringing her straight to Small, I mean.'

'We aim to please,' Molly replied as the couple continued along the beach. 'But if Mr O'Hara died at three o'clock . . .'

'Or earlier.'

'Or earlier, then whoever Sarah saw wasn't the murderer.'

'May not have been the murderer.'

'But you said . . .'

'What I said was strictly for your information.'

'Yes, sir – I shan't tell a living soul. Promise. Anyway, I've forgotten, so tell me again.'

'O'Hara died from heart failure induced by a curarin injection in his left thigh administered between one-thirty – which is the last time Peregrine saw him – and three a.m. It couldn't have been any later because otherwise he'd have bled all over the place when his head was cut off.'

'Ugh.'

'Yes, not very nice, but there it is. The point is, the decapitation took place at least two and a half hours after the fellow died. That doesn't mean to say . . .'

'It couldn't have been the same person – I mean who did the injection and the . . . er . . . the other thing.' Molly nodded. 'No, I see all that, but why take the risk of coming back; or why not –' she paused again, then added with a shudder – 'cut his head off straight away?'

'Our theory is there were two people involved. What we're not certain of is whether they were acting independently.'

'Or as a ghoulish team. What a quite unbelievable place this is. Nuns shoving pot, maniacs with hypodermics, people mutilating dead bodies.'

'I'm not sure yet about the nuns.'

'You mean you'll keep an open mind till after the convent orgy.'

Treasure countered with a withering glance – quite lost on his wife who was looking the other way. 'I mean I left Small and the Customs chap knee deep in shredded cigars, and all they'd found was tobacco. The really curious thing was Paul O'Hara's reaction. Apparently he was furious when they seized his cargo – complained to the Governor, raised hell with Joyce. Then when they started the search he as good as said that if there was ganga in the cigars he'd been made an innocent dupe.'

'But there wasn't any ganga.'

'Not up to the point where I left. You'd have thought O'Hara would have been relieved.'

'Or more furious.'

Treasure nodded. 'Or both – but he was neither. He looked to me to be in a state of shock.'

'What's curarin?' Molly switched the conversation back to an area where perfidy had been evidenced more clearly.

'The active ingredient in curare. It's a vegetable extract.'

'Like Marmite?' – Molly's favourite breakfast spread.

'Not quite. It's the stuff the Indians used to put on poisoned arrows – maybe they still do. Anyway, it's the first thing they test for out here when they run a poison check.'

'Why did they think Mr O'Hara was poisoned?'

'They didn't. Not at first, that is. They had his medical history, and once they'd established he couldn't have died from decapitation they thought he'd had a heart attack. The obvious symptoms fitted, apparently.'

'You mean he hadn't turned green from the vegetables or anything?'

'No, but I gather some of his organs were too rigid.'

'Really.' Molly drew out the word. 'So that's what curare does. I'll bet Mrs Dogwall never travels without some.'

'Very droll,' Treasure observed drily. 'D'you want to hear the rest?'

'Yes, please, I think you policemen are marvellous.'

'Well, they did the routine poison checks and came up with curarin first go. Like marijuana, you can grow your own in this part of the world, apparently – though I imagine you need to know a bit about botany.'

Molly was serious again. 'So if poor Mr O'Hara hadn't lost his head . . . sorry, I mean . . .'

'If it hadn't been for that I doubt there'd have been an autopsy – in fact I know there wouldn't. Small said as much.'

'So your two arch criminals were working against each other.'

'Mm, or just unknown to each other.'

'That's what I meant. How do you inject somebody with something without his screaming blue murder?'

'Any number of ways if the subject's asleep.'

'You mean you put a pillow over his head and ask him to hold still when he wakes up?'

Treasure thought for a moment. 'Something like that, perhaps. Remember that TV programme we saw about the Circadian cycle?'

'No.'

'Yes you do,' he insisted with a touch of impatience. 'It was about the times of day when one's metabolism is least resistent to strain, and . . .'

'Oh yes. They said that was why most heart attacks happen in the middle of the night – and you were frightened to go to bed for weeks after.'

'I was nothing of the sort.'

'Well, you kept taking your pulse at the most extraordinary times.'

'That's the point – or nearly – according to the autopsy report. I saw the telex. O'Hara had very bad angina. Somebody stuck a huge shot of curarin into him when his body was least able to take a shock. A strong dose of the stuff apparently paralyses the lungs. Well, obviously it would do for O'Hara quicker than for most people.' Treasure paused. 'Yes, you might have to use a pillow – or a pad over his mouth, but not for very long.'

'But surely he'd have made some sort of noise.'

'Perhaps, but not enough to wake Peregrine.'

'Who was at the bottom of *his* Circadian cycle,' Molly offered knowingly.

'Who would have been in a very deep sleep since he hadn't had any to speak of for twenty-four hours.'

'He says something woke him at five-thirty.'

'The second visitation – the one Sarah saw. Incidentally, that clears Peregrine completely in Small's eyes, thank heaven.'

'But surely he never seriously thought . . .'

'No, but if a local copper had been in charge he'd have

been perfectly entitled to hold the boy on suspicion – and probably would have done.'

'Just because he was there?' Molly demanded incredulously.

'During both crimes, remember.'

'And stayed so everyone would know. He wouldn't have been so stupid.'

Treasure was far from convinced about the last point but he let it pass. 'He didn't stay. He ran like hell.'

'That was afterwards. Anyway, you said he's in the clear. What about all the other suspects? Do they really have alibis?'

'Most people are in bed between one and three in the morning tucked up with witnesses.'

'Including this good Father Babington? All part of the convent service . . .'

'No, Babington was by himself.'

'And Joe O'Hara's brother – he's a bachelor, isn't he?'

'But not a celibate, apparently.'

'Oo, how juicy. Was he shacked up with a floozy?'

'I shouldn't tell you.'

'But you're going to because we have absolutely no secrets from each other.' She squeezed his arm. 'Come on, dish the dirt.'

'He says he was entertaining the Buckingham House kitchen maid.' There was doubt in Treasure's tone.

'How boring – and not necessarily convincing. If she's anything like Sarah, she'd probably say whatever he told her.'

'We had the same idea – but there's corroboration of a sort. He's been exercising seigneurial rights with this particular female for some time – says she's the reason he stays at the house when he's here. He certainly didn't go there to enjoy his brother's company. He could have stayed on the yacht.'

Molly drew a long face. 'Sounds fishy to me. Anyway, your fiendishly clever plan is going to smoke out the villain.'

They were drawing close to the guest-house. 'It could do, and Small wants to give it a try. He's precious little else to go on, poor chap.'

'Then tell me . . .'

'I'm not telling you any more because I don't want you any more involved.' This time Treasure was serious. 'But you're to do as I say. Don't leave Government House for any reason at all after dinner. I shall be disappearing, but you'll have plenty of company.'

'The Dogwalls are being moved up there.'

Treasure nodded. 'At Small's request to Rees – for their own safety. It'll be a bit of a squash, apparently.'

'Which shouldn't bother Mrs Dogwall,' Molly said archly. 'What about Peregrine?'

'We're short-handed so he'll be with me.' This was the only part of the plan Treasure contemplated with misgiving. 'In the circumstances, Small only trusts a handful of his policemen.'

The couple stopped at the paved way that led from the beach to the guest-house. Treasure studied the elevation of the long bungalow with more interest than its plain appearance seemed to warrant.

'That hole in the wall is where Peregrine's air-conditioner used to live,' Molly remarked with a smile.

'Mm, and the door and window next to it on the end must be Sarah's domain.' Treasure turned to his wife. 'Now, I'm seeing Paul O'Hara at six and Joyce after that, so I'll need to get moving. Just behave normally. I'll be back before dinner. You can tell me then who pumps you hardest for information.'

'And much good it may do them since you've hardly told me anything. By the way, if I'm to be left unprotected you might tell me whether I'm in danger of being injected or just beheaded.'

Treasure smiled. 'Neither in your case. Anyway, there won't be any more beheadings.'

'Why not?'

'You can work that out for yourself. There's nothing new in the world except the history you don't know.' Treasure added absently, 'Harry Truman said that, but no one was listening to him either: not at the time.'

CHAPTER XVIII

Paul O'Hara had recaptured some of the ebullience Treasure had been led to expect in him.

'Can I get you another drink?'

The banker declined the offer. The two were standing on the flag-stoned terrace of Buckingham House.

'You didn't mind my mentioning the girl? Chief Inspector Small hesitated to ask you.'

O'Hara affected diffidence. 'Well, you can tell him I'm not on intimate terms with every young female on the island – much as that may surprise him. He obviously told you about the girl here.' Treasure gave no sign of comprehension. 'If he'd been on the island longer he'd be less shocked by the prevailing moral mores.' O'Hara took a long gulp from the glass in his hand. 'On the other hand, perhaps he wouldn't. Prissy old devil, seems to me – on a par with my revered brother. And this girl Sarah claims she saw someone enter and leave the cabin?'

It seemed to Treasure that the enquiry had been a little too casual. 'Yes, but as I said, she's very vague about the whole thing – or perhaps apprehensive about naming names.'

'But she was camped outside the whole night?'

'Apparently so – and never plucked up the courage to go in.' Treasure had told the story as he and Small had agreed it should be retailed to O'Hara and others. 'The Chief Inspector still thinks she may have recognized the caller, but is too frightened to say so. He felt if we could find someone she knows and trusts . . .'

'Maybe she'd spill the beans? I wouldn't count on it,

Treasure. If you want my opinion she's cooked up the whole thing to get attention – or money. Did she ask for money?'

'Not that I know of.'

O'Hara took another drink. He sniggered. 'It could be Joe had offered her money to sleep with him, she held out hoping he'd up the ante, and now it's too late she's trying for something in compensation.'

'Is it likely she'd have . . . er . . . held out? You said . . .'

'That most of the local girls enjoy a tumble in the hay with the gentry? That's true, but if you'd known Joe you could understand why there was never a queue. If this trollop was hesitating in the bushes she was figuring out the prices for the menu – and very possibly deciding not to be the dish of the day after all.' O'Hara debated the credibility of this conjecture in his own mind. 'Anyway, I don't know the girl so it's not likely she'll unburden to me. I'd still guess the whole thing's a fabrication.'

'I think Small's come to the same conclusion,' Treasure gave a relaxed smile. 'But he still has the idea she may come cleaner when she's slept on it. It did take her some hours to come forward in the first place. Meantime he's sent her home.'

'To look after the Dogwalls.' O'Hara had his back to Treasure. He was refilling his glass at the small drinks table laid out on the terrace. It was difficult to judge whether the speaker was truly seeking enlightenment.

'To get some rest actually – she's tired out.' Treasure did not want to leave room for doubt. 'I gather the Dog-walls are departing in the morning.'

O'Hara turned and nodded. 'Which reminds me, I'm casting off myself in an hour.' He looked towards the unnaturally darkening southern horizon. 'Feel it getting sticky? There's an electric storm on the way.' He paused. 'Think over that proposition.'

Treasure smiled. 'I will.'

Earlier the banker had humoured O'Hara by allowing him to outline a new business deal involving the cigar company and the distillery project. This had differed from the plan proposed by Joe O'Hara in one important particular: it involved heavy front-loading in cash payments to Paul O'Hara in return for greater freedom of action and lower long-term costs in other contexts. Treasure had already concluded the proposition smelled too strongly of get-rich-quick ambitions on the part of his present companion: this was not the time, however, to say as much.

Surprisingly – or so it seemed to Treasure – the dead man's brother had shown little interest in discussing the fatality. He had been told by Small earlier that the results of the autopsy would not be available until the following day, but the first investigations suggested a heart attack had been the cause of death. O'Hara had made the single caustic observation to Treasure that he had reached the same conclusion without benefit of a medical degree. After that he had let the subject drop – and with no comment on the still unexplained decapitation.

The banker put down his glass. 'Well, I must leave you to lock up the shop. Oh, you'll keep the business of the girl to yourself?' O'Hara nodded unconcernedly. 'I'll walk down through the garden, if that's all right.'

'Sure, just follow the path off the drive. I'll be back tomorrow or the next day. As for locking up the place, it's more necessary than you'd guess,' O'Hara continued pointedly. 'Joe's servants have been robbing him for years – God knows what they'll start lifting with no one in residence. And that goes for several thousand others in the vicinity.'

This jaundiced view of the honesty of Carleons hardly fitted with the facts as Treasure knew them. 'But you'll have staff about the place?'

'In their own quarters without access to the main rooms – and that's the way they'll stay until I've got an up-to-date inventory. The place will be as burglar-proof as I can make it.'

Treasure took his leave, privately marvelling at the

tolerance of a certain kitchen maid whose normal incarceration in the scullery was relieved by occasional but short-lived promotions to pleasuring in the master-bedroom. Feudalism appeared to be alive and well on KCI: or was it? His mind turned to the man who was next on his calling list.

O'Hara watched the banker out of sight, then stepped through the open french windows into the library. He locked the windows behind him and pocketed the key. He had not brought Treasure into this room. The two tea-chests near the door into the hall might have witnessed that the sack of Buckingham House had already started – in a selective way: one contained six valuable, if little known, paintings of the French Impressionist School: the other was full of Georgian silver. Both cases would be decently shrouded on their journey down to the quayside. Their contents could be expected to produce a substantial price on the American market, even if they had to be offered without a completely respectable provenance – a possibility their vendor would accept philosophically since he was planning to be paid for them twice.

O'Hara moved to the desk. Some of the papers there he took to the safe. One document he folded carefully before putting it in the inside pocket of his blazer. He had lost one small fortune that day in the incinerator's smoke.

If he was honest with himself, he had to admit that Babington's duplicity had probably saved them both from prison. It also meant that he was shipping a virtually worthless load of cigars – a load that had satisfied the KCI Customs Authority but which was unlikely to satisfy anybody else.

Joe had never confided in Paul that the nuns had always kept stored a sufficient quantity of 'unfortified' Elegantes to meet precisely the emergency they had faced that day. Even so, it had not been necessary for Babington to order the destruction of more than a million dollars' worth of highly marketable merchandise when he had told the nuns to make the switch. The stuff could have been hidden. They were plenty of places in a convent from which even authorized searchers could be barred – the space in the chapel behind the altar frontal, for instance. Paul O'Hara had never been much touched by religion.

It was some compensation that Joe's propensity for over-caution could be turned to account in just one context. Only a fool would have insured this Victorian barn at all – and only a raving idiot would have had the valuation of the building and its contents indexed to UK prices. But Joe had done just that – and paid the premiums before the due date like the good little bourgeois he was. O'Hara tapped his pocket: he had the policy and receipt to prove the matter.

'There's no way we'll force the girl to remember, Mr Treasure. No way.' Mongo Joyce added a touch of vehemence to the impartial observation. It was as though the security of his all-night alibi licensed some overt strengthening to the objectivity of the assertion. 'Of course I'll see her if Small wants. I know her – but only very slightly.' He cast a glance at his wife.

Mrs Joyce had remained present throughout Treasure's visit. The banker had been glad of this, and had been carefully noting the plump young matron's reactions to her husband's pronouncements. If the last disclaimer had been intended as some kind of reassurance she had greeted it impassively. The wronged wife lacked nothing in dignity while presiding in her own living-room.

The room – like the house – was neat but uninteresting. There were no pictures or books, the furnishings were new without being modern, as though they had survived unscathed from that unnamed era – post-utilitarian but pre-Design Council – loved only by junk men.

The Joyce domestic scene was singularly lacking in cultured as well as cultural amenity. Treasure was seated in the centre of it without feeling that he had reached the heart. He found himself speculating on the type of comfort – material and intellectual as well as emotional – provided for the Chief Minister further down the street. Involuntarily he smoothed the arm of his chair: he doubted Lady Cynthia Franks-Barrett much favoured uncut moquette.

'Mr Small thinks the girl knows more than she's telling?' Mrs Joyce enquired.

Treasure shrugged. 'It's difficult to say. If she really did see somebody it's strange she can't offer the remotest kind of description.'

'I think my husband should see her – but tomorrow as you say.' The words came more as an injunction than a suggestion – and they were clearly addressed to Joyce himself: he reacted with a nod of agreement.

The two had been more concerted than Treasure had expected – and Mrs Joyce a good deal more assured than he had imagined, following the description Small had offered of this wife in name only. The banker speculated on the reason for the likely metamorphosis he was witnessing.

'Meantime, the Chief Inspector would be grateful if we'd keep the matter to ourselves.' Treasure gave an embarrassed smile. 'Incidentally, you'd be perfectly right in judging all this is none of my business. It's simply that Sarah poured her heart out to my wife . . .'

'And Small very sensibly recruited you as a disinterested go-between.' The understanding in Joyce's voice was measured and – to a tuned ear – calculated.

'He's up to his eyes in work.' Treasure rose to take his leave.

Joyce moved to the door. 'If the formal autopsy report confirms Joe died of a heart attack he should be less busy tomorrow.'

Treasure nodded. 'There's still the matter of the decapitation, of course, which . . .'

'Which will probably have to remain unexplained even if its symbolism is understood.' The Chief Minister sounded curiously philosophical. 'I don't condone the mutilation, Mr Treasure. It was a sacrilegious action – but as a crime one feels it belongs in the body-snatching category.' He waited while Treasure shook hands with his wife. 'I'm glad you're not cutting your stay short. I look forward to our business meeting tomorrow – which will also be in confidence.'

The banker had assumed the indulgent way he had been received had been coloured by political expediency. The last statement confirmed the point.

After seeing Treasure to the door, Joyce returned to the living-room and carefully re-read the copy of the telex report he had taken from his pocket. It had been delivered to him earlier through a very private channel and was a facsimile of the one addressed to Small setting out the cause of Joe O'Hara's death. The opportunity for circumspection on KCI was less complete than the visiting Chief Inspector might imagine – in this and other contexts. The Chief Minister shrugged his shoulders.

Mrs Joyce brushed past her husband. She was tight-lipped but more resolute than she had been in years. The charade was over – and it was going to stay over.

Treasure turned left out of the side-road to hurry the short distance to Government House and almost collided with Luke Murphy who was wheeling his bicycle in the other direction.

'D'you always push it downhill, Mr Murphy?' Treasure asked with a smile.

'It don' ever rain but what it pours, sah – and it's gonna do just dat before long.' The black man looked up at the sky before fixing Treasure with a broad grin. 'Fust off, me gotta fix a damn puncture in de back tyre – den me gonna get *Sir Dafydd* runnin' like a bird ready fo' yo' 'naugral trip tomorrow.'

'My trip?'

'Yes, sah. Is de Governor's plan fo' a quiet picnic lunch on Mount Manitou for you an' yo' lady – bein' yo' seen nothin' yet of dis lovely island.'

'Sounds delightful – but I'm sorry if it means you'll . . .'

'Be workin' on de railroad all evenin'.' Luke slapped his

side in huge delight. 'My pleasure, sah. Dat old engine's me pride an' joy – and His Excellency's. It's bes' we keep her fired tonight.'

Treasure examined the almost black cloud-line to seaward; it was strangely threatening – even unnerving to a stranger watching a curtain of darkness advance upon an already unnaturally orange sky. 'Well, stay in the dry,' he called after the retreating figure.

Alibi or no alibi, it was impossible to credit that the mild-mannered Murphy had chopped off Joe O'Hara's head. Yet Sarah had at first seemed so certain.

In any event, things appeared to be going according to plan, and Small had evidently been as conscientious as Treasure in setting about his planned series of interviews and arrangements.

It had been Treasure's idea to have Murphy occupied all evening at the engine shed – a safe distance from Government House. As he walked up the incline the banker was in time to see Paul O'Hara's yacht clearing the harbour and heading westwards. It had also been his suggestion that O'Hara should not be hindered in his desire to leave that evening. He glanced at his watch. It was seven-thirty – a bit early to expect developments but with the light fading so fast it was as well that everyone would be taking up his station.

It was some satisfaction that for the next few hours at least Treasure's own allotted responsibility was to observe the reactions and movements of those others invited to dine with the Governor.

CHAPTER XIX

Amos, the butler, turned off the lights in the drawing-room of Government House plunging the assembled company into total darkness. He then began to feel his way back to the projector – a task made no easier by the effects of his having consumed the quite considerable quantity of port remaining in the decanter after dinner.

'Amos, you're holding my knee. Pull yourself together.' Lady Rees was not amused.

Moments later a flapping noise indicated that Amos, still off course, was doing battle with the portable screen. The lights came on again and Debby was revealed standing by the switches. 'Go back to the projector, Amos. I'll work the lights when you're ready.'

'Are you sure you want to see this film, Molly?' Lady Rees turned to her companion on the sofa which constituted – with an armchair – the front row of the makeshift cinema. 'I mean, you've probably seen it a dozen times before – I know I have. Not that that matters to me one bit. Archie keeps hiring it because of the train – oh, and he once met Alec Guinness. I expect you know all the important actors. There's nothing much to do here in the evenings. I'd have organized bridge but –' the diatribe continued, only the tone was lowered in deference to the occupant of the armchair – 'the Dogwalls don't play. He, would you believe it, suggested some kind of poker.' There was a temporary cessation in the breathless soliloquy to permit the proper savouring of the last-advertised social solecism.

'Strip poker?' Molly Treasure enquired in an earnest tone.

Lady Rees's mouth fell open and her eyebrows lifted; this gave her the appearance of a surprised hippopotamus.

'You think Sawah will be okay down there by herself?' The lull in the conversation to her left had prompted Mrs Dogwall to lean across Molly and to address her apparently stupefied hostess. 'I mean, maybe she could use some pwotection – being she knows . . .'

'I'm sure the district nurse or somebody will be looking in on her.' It was Molly who answered. 'But remember, what Mark said at dinner was very privileged information. Nobody else knows that Sarah thinks she saw the prowler.' Molly smiled reassuringly. 'And as Mark emphasized, when it came to the point her memory – or her imagination – seemed quite to give out on her.'

'You think she cooked up the whole stowy?'

'Such things have been known. Is your husband not joining us, Mrs Dogwall?' Molly glanced over her shoulder at the second row of assorted chairs. Only one was occupied – by the Governor who was absently studying Mrs Dogwall's bare back over the top of his coffee cup.

'Oh, he'll be down in a minute. He's calling home.'

'That could take all evening.' Lady Rees re-entered the conversation but without making it plain whether she was referring to the verbosity of Glen Dogwall or the shortcomings of the KCI telephone system. She had concluded the surmise about the strip poker had been ill-judged – but not before her *alter ego* had perversely forced her to calculate the sum of her garments, as well as to estimate that Mrs Dogwall's matching total probably came to one. 'Archie, are we really not to wait for Mark?' She had strained her neck through ninety degrees and broken into her husband's reverie with an accusing stare as well as the staccato question.

'He's gone to see Small, my dear.'

'Then let's start the film.'

Amos, the object of this last command, prepared to obey, steeling himself to operate the 16mm projector with the studied ignorance of a householder searching for a gas leak with a lighted match.

Debby extinguished the lights and the audience was treated to its promised exhibition of *The Bridge Over the River Kwai* – beginning with reel two, and firmly out of focus.

It was several minutes before Amos's tentative adjustments to most parts of the machine, ending with the lens, served to confirm the error in sequence. Since the ensuing reel change necessitated re-illumination of the whole scene, Molly Treasure was able to note that the Governor had already decided to eschew the opportunity to watch his favourite moving picture. He had left the room.

'Ten past ten and all's well.' Treasure had located Small in the appointed spot – under a bread-fruit tree in the garden of Government House.

'Nothing's happened – but the rain's held off at least.' Small was bulkier but prepared in a plastic mackintosh.

'My bit went all right,' said Treasure cheerfully. 'I saw O'Hara and the Joyces as arranged, and I let the story out casually during dinner. Debby nearly upset the apple cart by announcing she'd look in on Sarah later.'

'Oh lord. Did you head her off, sir?'

'My wife did – said Sarah'd been given a sedative and put to bed.' Treasure settled himself on the grass beside the Chief Inspector. He looked about him. 'Pity the night's so dark, but you were right – this is the best vantage point.'

From where they were sitting the two men commanded a view forward both of the Governor's residence and the guest-house. To the left they could dimly discern the main drive to the house and to the right the white surf on an open stretch of beach.

'My lot bought it hook, line and sinker.' Small gave a satisfied grunt. 'Babington thought he might have some influence with Sarah – said he'd see her in the morning. McLush had that chap Brown with him – very agitated he was. He doesn't know Sarah, but he seemed relieved I was letting him into my confidence . . .'

'And off the hook?'

'Something like that, yes. Asked if he could interview Sarah.'

'Pushing his luck, wasn't he?'

'That's what I thought, and said so. I told him he wasn't to go near her without my permission and that I'd want to see him for further questioning in the morning.' Small paused. 'How did you explain away Mr Gore, sir?'

'Said he was suffering delayed exhaustion, that he'd gone to bed in my dressing-room and didn't want to be disturbed. I assume he's in position?'

'Since eight o'clock. I've got two of my sergeants down there as well. Are you still backing your hunch?'

Treasure sighed. 'More than ever – but I hope I'm wrong. How d'you get on at the hospital?'

Small snorted with disgust. 'While I was waiting for the almoner I could have helped myself to a boat-load of dangerous drugs. Place is wide open. They're short-handed, of course, but that's no excuse for sloppy security. She had curarin – in ampoules, with none missing so far as she knew. I asked about other drugs first. She caught on pretty quickly. Asked if Mr O'Hara had done himself in with an overdose of sleeping pills.'

'With a heart condition I suppose he might have.' Treasure stopped short in mid-sentence. 'Good heavens, what's that?' he exclaimed pointing up the hill ahead.

Small was already heaving himself to his feet. 'That's the tower of Buckingham House, sir. And it's burning nicely by the look of it.'

The track-suited figure crouched in the foliage skirting the drive – on the far side from where Treasure and Small had been – came too late to see the two men pound off in the direction of the blaze.

To the new arrival the fire was almost unbelievably providential. Its attraction would surely remove the risk of any casual encounter in the garden. Sarah's room was still some distance, and it remained to be seen whether guards were posted there – but at least the route should be clear.

The church bell began to toll – the traditional summons for members of the KCI volunteer fire brigade. Relaxed by the diversion, but no less alert, the figure darted across the drive in the direction of the guest-house.

The swimmer in the wet suit hauled himself back into the inflatable dinghy. He paused for a moment to catch his breath, gazing across the hundred yards of water to the shoreline and beyond. Contentedly he watched the flames lick the lower windows of the tower half a mile to the west of where he had moored. There was no need to use the oars again as he had done for the last part of the inward journey – in another minute or so no one would be looking out to sea. He hauled up the drag anchor and applied himself to the starter cord of the outboard motor.

Two minutes later the dinghy was moving slowly westwards, throttle well back. The occupant set a course for the end of the stone harbour breakwater. He heard the ringing of the church bell at the same moment as he sighted the MS *Joseph O'Hara* rounding the mole. The three men who crewed KCI's spanking new fire launch had waited two months to prove their alacrity. Their hoses might not reach to the site of the emergency but this unproved conjecture paled beside the extent of their aspirations. With searchlight roaming and siren blaring the *Joseph O'Hara* was heading for a real fire at last.

The man in the dinghy swore aloud and swung the tiller to head inshore. With luck the fools wouldn't sight him. He opened the throttle and raced for the shelter of the harbour wall. Seconds later he cursed his stupidity – and the motor he had wrecked.

The screw of the dinghy hit the coral outcrop at the exact moment the heavens were rent by the longest vein of lightning Peregrine had ever seen. He happened also to be looking out to sea from his uncomfortable sentry position behind the hole in his bathroom wall.

It was the fire launch that had first attracted Peregrine's attention, but it was the lightning that illuminated one of the things Treasure had warned him to look for – a dinghy conceivably heading for the beach house.

Huge spots of rain began to fall as Peregrine raced out into the open. Without thinking, eagerly he waved the beam of the heavy duty torch across the surface of the sea until he picked up the dinghy. The occupant was flailing the water with oars, rowing with the tide towards the breakwater. 'Got you,' the junior banker said aloud – and

then remembered Treasure's injunction: under no circumstances was any intruder to be alerted until it could be
established without doubt that he was aiming to break into
Sarah's room.

Even as Peregrine recalled his orders, the oarsman
turned his head momentarily in the direction of the torch
beam, then returned to pulling hard for the shore.
Obviously he knew he had been spotted. His subsequent
action would indicate his guilt or innocence, and Peregrine
determined to be on hand for the revelation – difficult as it
might be to ascribe criminal intent to anyone stoutly
maintaining his status as a passing boatman.

He addressed a bush at the side of the house. 'Sergeant,
I'm going after that man.' Predictably the bush made no
reply. 'Sergeant, where are you?' Peregrine loudly
harangued a whole line of bushes.

'Here, sah.' The sergeant appeared from a clump that
had promised better protection from the rain than his
original station had offered.

Peregrine thrust the torch into the man's hands. 'Keep
the light on the chap in the boat. He's coming ashore.
Tell the Chief Inspector where I've gone.'

It was barely three hundred yards along the sand to the
breakwater, and while Peregrine covered the distance at
speed, the alerted wet-suited figure had abandoned the
dinghy, waded to the beach, and was a full minute ahead
of his pursuer by the time both had gained the flat of
Rupertstown's long quayside. At least it was clear the man
was acting suspiciously. He had taken no notice of Peregrine's bellowed order to stop. He could, of course, be
deaf, careless about his property, and in a hurry to get out
of the rain – but, on the whole, he seemed worth chasing.

The road to the right was alive with activity. People and
vehicles were pouring along its length in the direction of
the fire, undeterred by the now torrential rain. A fire-
engine – with the ubiquitous Luke Murphy at the wheel –
was splashing a way through the throng.

Despite the reducing visibility, Peregrine picked out the

fleeing figure where he estimated it would be – half-way along the well-lit quay and very nearly abreast of the railway yard. As he set off in pursuit the man appeared to hesitate, glanced back, then darted to the right. Peregrine changed direction to take the advantage offered, but seconds later his heart fell as he discerned the man's objective.

Standing in a siding to the nearside of the engine shed, its line of egress unobstructed, was the convent rail trolley.

The man had mounted the trolley and had started to pump its operating lever before Peregrine had covered half the distance between them. The trolley began to move away at barely walking pace. Peregrine kept on running – it was becoming a habit. He was still making better speed than the trolley, still closing fast on his quarry – when he slipped on the cobbled ground and fell on his face. He was up again quickly, shaken but unhurt – but the advantage had been lost. Despite the under-crewing, the trolley was now gliding along at better than twelve miles an hour and gaining in momentum by the second.

Wishing he had been paying more attention to Luke Murphy's discourse the night before, Peregrine opened the steam regulator lever, wound down the brake-block handwheel at the back of the cab, and set *Sir Dafydd* moving briskly – towards the rear of the engine shed. Thanks to the excessive steam power released by its untutored operator, the driving wheels began slipping and the locomotive lost traction before hitting the buffers. Peregrine reapplied the brakes, shut off the steam, and racked the pivoted reversing rod into the forward position. Shortly afterwards, *Sir Dafydd* was making fairly smooth progress in the right direction, albeit at the speed only of a healthy carthorse, due to shortage of steam pressure and another inhibiting factor.

Peregrine had dived into the deserted engine shed in search of help. The presence of the softly hissing, gleaming *Sir Dafydd* had seemed heaven-sent. He regretted the

precious time wasted mastering the controls – or very
nearly mastering them. He had stuffed the firebox full of
wood from the bunker on the left. Since the boiler gauges
were meaningless to him he elected to ignore them. The
pressure gauge on the cabside to the right he assumed was
some kind of speedometer. Peregrine's approach to
engine-driving was enthusiastically pragmatic.

Whoever was ahead on the trolley had a three- or four-
minute start, and judging by the speed the engine was
making the fugitive's lead was unlikely to be much reduced.
It was some consolation that the two line-locked vehicles
had to be heading for the same destination. Rain completely obscured the view through the glazed forward
portholes of the cabin. Either Peregrine and whoever he
was pursuing were making for the end of the line, or else
Sir Dafydd would be running into the abandoned trolley
without warning. Peregrine mentally prepared for either
eventuality: the physical and mechanical effects would
have to depend on circumstances – or fate.

Ten minutes later and some four miles along the line the
exhausted occupant of the trolley braked the vehicle,
dismounted, and stumbled forward to the points. He
dragged at the little-used lever until in response to a super-
human effort he felt and heard the track re-lock into
position. The noise of the steam-engine had grown
progressively louder since he had first become aware of it
some time earlier. It could only mean he was being
pursued in an unexpected but unquestionably efficient way.

The remedy was a drastic one, but the man was
undeterred. He propelled the trolley-car over the points
and on to the Gull Rock spur. He then got down again and
hurried back to the points lever. This time it was easier to
operate, and in any case he wrenched it through only half
its arc.

The tower of Buckingham House showed licking flames at
every window through all its stages: the east wing, too,

was well ablaze. Apart from a knot of frightened servants, Treasure and Small had been first on the scene and had supervised an elementary fire-fighting operation before the arrival of official forces.

The wide terrace was littered with furniture and other impedimenta hastily rescued from the west wing of the house. Treasure wondered whether the effort had been worth it since what had been spared from the maw of the widening conflagration seemed destined to be despoiled by the drenching rain.

With KCI's land and sea-borne fire brigades now doing their best to stop the flames from spreading, Small was applying himself to the more familiar and urgent task of herding sightseers to safety.

'When the frame of that tower's burnt through, the whole thing will collapse,' Treasure shouted to the Chief Inspector over the din of the activity all around them. 'The rain should save the outbuildings, but I think the house has had it.'

The scene was hard to credit – teeming rain on the outside and the updraught from the lower openings of the tower feeding the surging inferno inside. The firemen, hampered by the elements, inadequate equipment and too little experience, were concentrating on saturating the inside of the west wing.

'Sergeant, what are you doing here?' Small wheeled round at the sight of a uniformed figure making uneven progress towards him over trailing hoses and furniture.

The man saluted. 'Mr Gore, sah, he gone chasing someone comin' ashore like you expected. Man in a dinghy, sah. He said to tell you, sah . . .'

'When?'

'Five minutes, sah' – a not strictly accurate report since the sergeant had certainly spent more than that amount of time coming the long and obstructed way in the shelter of a hooded Land-Rover instead of racing up from the beach on foot.

Treasure had heard the exchange. 'So who's down at

the beach house?'

'Sergeant Riley, sah, he's still there . . .'

'Then you get back as quick as you can move. Mr Treasure, you want to go too . . . ?'

But Treasure had not waited for Small's question. He was already making off down the hill at the trot, uncertain that by the sergeant's definition Peregrine was chasing the right person.

CHAPTER XX

The drenched figure in the dark track-suit moved silently to the group of shrubs closest to the beach side of the house. It was clear the place was not under observation; so Mr Mark Treasure and his Chief Inspector friend were as ingenuous as they had seemed.

The careful search for watchers in the garden had been fruitless but necessary. It had also unknowingly been conducted after all but one of the appointed sentinels had left their posts to chase fires or suspected miscreants.

If only last night had been like this one – pitch dark, with torrential rain instead of cloudless with a full moon. If the girl had been at the cabin she must have recognized who she had seen. That she had not admitted as much so far was no assurance for the future – a sense of awe and respect, even of natural fear, could wear out; it could even be worn down by interrogation methods less mild than those likely to have been used so far.

If Sarah had been given a sedative there should be no struggle – but the knife would be quicker than curarin; the gun would have been more efficient still – but noisy, and riskier since it was a registered firearm. The door to Sarah's room was clearly visible under the porch light. It was a frame door with four louvred panels; it would not be locked, though it might be bolted from the inside. Try the door first and if that failed go in through the window –

the window that was conveniently open.

Half blinded by the torrent of rain, Peregrine had been hanging out through the left-hand side of the engine cab doing his best to see what lay ahead. He knew he must soon be approaching a set of points. To his sudden surprise and innocent, short-lived delight, he made out the branch line snaking off to Gull Rock with the trolley-car not fifty yards along it. The fugitive had obviously stopped to change the points: it was not immediately clear he had done so twice. This last realization registered with Peregrine at the moment *Sir Dafydd*'s front driving wheels hit the half-open points. The little engine gave a huge lurch to the right, then literally bounced back to the left. Momentum and an almost human capacity for dealing with the eccentricities of KCI's iron road kept the more than a century old steamer on the track. After almost tipping its driver out of the cab *Sir Dafydd* puffed triumphantly onwards towards Mount Manitou – much to the chagrin of the watcher on the convent trolley.

It was a credit to Peregrine's improving quality as an engineer that twice to stop *Sir Dafydd* and twice to change the points lost him only half a mile to the exhausted man on the trolley.

The rain now suddenly ceased – almost as abruptly as it had started. A watery moon was illuminating the way ahead. With predictable ease *Sir Dafydd* was closing on the little rail car. This was new territory to Peregrine but he remembered McLush's description of how the branch line ended – and the stricture about the rotting viaduct to the island. Perhaps he should stop the engine on the mainland and continue the pursuit on foot. He was now almost on top of the trolley but despite the obvious weariness of its operator the thing was still moving faster than even the revived Peregrine could hope to run.

It was then that Peregrine sighted the outline of a vessel he could not fail to recognize as O'Hara's yacht glistening in the moonlight and moored, it seemed, a few hundred yards up the line. It was the shock and portent of this sight that temporarily took his mind off matters of more immediate concern. This was unfortunate both because *Sir Dafydd* had now worked up a respectable head of pressure and also because Peregrine had for the first time – if inadvertently – released the steam brake by falling against this unrecognized object when he had been tossed across the cabin at the points.

The liberated engine lurched along the line at record speed. Too late, Peregrine applied himself to preventing his bucking mount from forsaking a land-locked life for the beckoning status of a boat train.

Sergeant Sammy Riley was wet and uncomfortable. Two and a half hours on the flat roof of the guest-house with no shelter and only a rifle for company had done nothing to improve his normally disgruntled and aggressive disposition. He wished now that he had taken a shot at the man in the dinghy – it would have been contrary to orders but he was a marksman, the best in the force. If the objective of this whole ill-explained exercise was to trap Uncle Joe's assassin – and Chief Inspector Small had virtually implied as much – one well-aimed bullet at a suspicious party behaving in exactly the way predicted of *the* guilty party would have saved a lot of trouble later. It would also have saved Sammy Riley getting any wetter and Sammy Riley's latest woman from going to waste on what should have been a holiday.

But the orders had been to shoot only after challenge – and you could hardly challenge someone nearly a quarter of a mile distant, with fire-boats sirening and church bells ringing, even though you were a good enough shot to lay a bead on him through rain and quivering torchlight.

The low retaining wall on the roof's edge had made Sergeant Riley invisible from any angle in the garden throughout his vigil. He had kept watch through the wide draining apertures. His field of vision covered the whole approach area in front of Sarah's room: obviously he could not see anyone who moved in flat against the wall immediately below him – that came in Sergeant Brough's designated area of surveillance, and when the track-suited figure used precisely that route to reach the door Sergeant Brough had gone to the fire.

Sammy Riley did not see the figure go in to Sarah's room, nor did he at first hear anything below. He did both feel and hear the thud of the door as it closed itself behind the figure now in full retreat and not caring about cover nor anything else save the quickest route to safety.

'Halt or I fire. Halt or I fire,' yelled Sammy – and fired.

'Stop! Don't shoot! Stop, Mrs Joyce!' cried Treasure as he raced around the building from behind. But he shouted too late.

'Lovely morning, Sir Archibald.' Small was aware that virtually every Caribbean morning was lovely, but you had to say something. He glanced expectantly at Treasure who was already seated at the Council Room table.

The Governor was slow to acknowledge the policeman's arrival. He turned his head in Small's direction, fixed him with a vacant stare which eventually gave place to an unexpected and sickly grin. He nodded towards a chair, then unconsciously let out a long sigh. Treasure smiled at Small in an attempt to indicate his appearance had coincided with rather than precipitated the audible sound of woe.

Rees was doing his best to shake off his preoccupation with what he kept telling himself was the most trivial event in the whole ghastly catalogue.

Joe O'Hara had been slain with an injection. The perpetrator of this outrage – the Chief Minister's wife no less – had been shot dead. Paul O'Hara was in hospital under arrest – and treatment for multiple injuries sustained through the too late abandoning of a stolen trolley-car that failed to bridge the gap between the end of a pier and the stern of a yacht. This last impossible feat had been attempted involuntarily: at the time the trolley was being propelled from the rear by a runaway, abandoned engine.

It would have been excusable if Her Majesty's representative on King Charles Island had relegated these incontrovertible happenings for later consideration and concentrated on eliciting whether his own massive, impulsive indiscretion had been discovered.

Yet perversely, in his mind's eye everything seemed to pale beside the picture of his beloved steam-engine sunk among the fishes off Gull Rock.

'We'll never get it up.' The Governor shook his head sadly. 'I was there at first light. Must have been going like a jet.' The analogy was somehow consoling: a valedictory tribute.

Small looked puzzled.

'We were talking about the steam-engine,' Treasure offered gently. 'Sir Archibald was surprised it got across the causeway to Gull Rock – the timbers of the viaduct are apparently just as rotten as the pier further on. That collapsed, of course.'

'Good thing Mr Gore jumped for it – could have been very nasty. Wonder the thing didn't explode.' Small also wondered why they had him discussing trains at a time like this.

'I doubt it would have occurred to Peregrine to go down with a sinking engine.' Treasure spoke lightly and without malice. Altogether Peregrine had retrieved as well as preserved himself. It was unlikely he would have been able to restrain the trigger-happy police sergeant if he had remained at the beach, so it was as well he had been engaged elsewhere at the time of the summary execution.

The Governor visibly stirred himself, 'That girl – Sarah – you say she didn't reach the lodge until five-thirty yesterday morning?'

'Or thereabouts.' Treasure marvelled at the time it had taken Rees to return to a subject of such primary importance.

'So she couldn't have seen the . . . the er . . .'

'She didn't see Mrs Joyce go in or come out. We just let Mrs Joyce and a number of others think she was there all night – or most of it.'

Rees abjured referring to the fact that he had been included among the others. 'You suspected Mrs Joyce?'

'Mr Treasure did, sir.' This was Small. 'My money was on Paul O'Hara.' There seemed no point in dissembling when he had earlier left O'Hara trussed and tractioned in the hospital, having charged the man with arson and advised him – in compensation – that he was lucky to be alive.

'O'Hara certainly had a motive for doing away with his brother – and he's a thoroughly nasty piece of work. Personally, I came to the conclusion he'd stop short of murder.' Treasure paused. 'Almost certainly he'd been blackmailing Joe for some time – over the cigar business.'

'The cigar business?' Rees appeared genuinely puzzled.

'It seems unlikely we're ever going to prove it, but it's a reasonable supposition that the popularity of King Charles Elegantes has been based on their heavy content of marijuana.'

'I don't believe it.'

'I didn't think you would. And no one else will either.' Treasure glanced sagely at Small. 'The fact is that the O'Haras and Father Babington have been operating a tight little ring in soft drugs for the Florida gentry for quite some time.'

'But they'll be found out.' Rees sounded more resigned than surprised. The modest exposure planned for that part of the British Commonwealth of Nations over which he held constitutional sway was promising to escalate into a full frontal revelation.

'Unlikely.' Treasure sounded matter-of-fact. 'There's no hard evidence left on the island, and when the American news media announce the sad condition of the O'Hara clan I doubt there'll be any in the USA either.'

'I don't follow.' This was an understatement: the

Governor metaphorically had hardly set out.

It was Small who interposed with his own theory. 'When Paul O'Hara's customers in the States hear he's in trouble – and his brother murdered – they'll likely assume it's something to do with their favourite cigars, sir. They're all monied, which in my experience means they'll not need lessons in self-preservation.' The Chief Inspector shot a half-apologetic glance at Treasure whose cynical grimace indicated tacit agreement with this raw empirical judgement. 'They'll know they're on a list the police could get hold of. Mr Treasure's right, sir. By tonight there won't be what he calls a fortified Elegante in existence anywhere.'

'But how have the O'Haras got away with it – as you say, for all these years?' The Governor was still trailing.

'Because it was in the interests of everybody involved to see that they did.' Treasure's tone was inconsequential. 'Lesser secrets have been kept by larger numbers.'

This remark registered with the Governor who happened to be a Freemason. 'But you said there was blackmail.'

On reflection Treasure now wished he had eschewed making that disclosure. It had been breakfast-time in Zürich – two a.m. on KCI – when he had made his second telephone call to the President of Grifer, Lerc. On that occasion, with the sure knowledge that Paul O'Hara had criminal charges to answer, he had been in a strong position to barter for information with Pierre Lerc. In the event, the Swiss banker had been extremely grateful for the intelligence that a client to whom he was just about to advance money against an expectancy could look forward not only to a severe drop in income but also to a probable period in jail. These were the kind of expectations that seriously altered the status of Grade A customers.

In return for this timely warning, Lerc confirmed that the numbered account into which Joseph O'Hara had been paying substantial amounts was not unconnected with a close relative.

Treasure had already revealed this confidence to Chief

Inspector Small on the understanding that it was in the cause of affirming McLush's innocence. He nodded at Rees. 'I said I think it probable Paul had been blackmailing his brother, but that too will be difficult if not impossible to prove. It shouldn't go any further.' Treasure was reassured by the knowledge that before the interview was over the Governor's total discretion promised to be forthcoming on all counts. 'Of course,' he continued, 'if Paul hadn't been so greedy Joe wouldn't have wanted to wind up the illegal but profitable element in the cigar business.'

'And that would have avoided all this . . . ?' The Governor's words were slow; the tone curiously sceptical.

'No, not the murder, nor of course the beheading.' Treasure was careful to observe the effect of his last words. The Governor's eyebrows had lifted perceptibly. 'The fact that he was being blackmailed about the cigars prompted Joe to write off the future in ganga – with Babington's reluctant but committed co-operation.' He glanced questioningly at Small.

'That's about it, Mr Treasure,' said the Chief Inspector. 'I've just finished breakfast with Father Babington – and very indigestible it was too. He's not admitting anything, but on the other hand he's not categorically denying much either. The situation was just as you figured it. He's still very depressed that Joe O'Hara wasn't letting him in to his confidence about his real intention on the future of the island – but he's thankful the murder had nothing to do with the cigar business.'

'So,' Treasure continued, 'if Paul hadn't been avaricious, yesterday morning he'd have inherited the cigar company – ganga and all. As it was, he needed Babington's continued co-operation for that to happen. But Babington had pledged his loyalty to Joe – at least in that connection. His denouncing Joe at the Mass was not to do with cigars or ganga.'

'And you've arrested Paul?' This fact had not been difficult for the Governor to recall since it was connected with a water-logged steam-engine.

'On a charge of arson with intent to defraud Lloyds of London of a quarter of a million pounds, sir.' As Small continued, Treasure privately wondered whether the very British policeman would have sounded quite so shocked if Buckingham House had been insured in some other national capital. 'He had the policy on him.' Small shook his head to emphasize what he evidently considered a bald extension to the perfidy. 'Of course, we'd have had difficulty nailing him if it hadn't been . . .'

'For Gore giving chase,'. the Governor interrupted solemnly. His words concerned Peregrine but his thoughts and sympathy lay with *Sir Dafydd* at the bottom of the ocean.

'Actually, no, sir. Oh, it was Mr Gore who apprehended him – in a manner of speaking, but all that proved was that O'Hara sneaked back to this area in a dinghy from the yacht that went no further than the Gull Rock pier.'

'It was his kitchen maid who turned him in.' This was Treasure. 'A woman slighted with a vengeance. In return for supplying home comforts over a considerable period, plus an alibi for the night before last, she'd demanded marriage in the near future and the run of the house from yesterday. O'Hara was daft enough to send her packing as part of his official leave-taking last evening – one of the reasons why he went to such pains locking up.'

'She came back, of course, probably intending to break in and pinch whatever was handy as some kind of compensation.' There was a most un-policeman-like implication in the Chief Inspector's tone that all things considered the girl's purpose was entirely justified. 'She saw O'Hara setting fire to the place and couldn't wait to tell me about it later.' Small paused, coughed nervously, and made a show of glancing at his watch. 'And now if you'll both excuse me, I've arranged to see Mr Joyce at ten o'clock – at his request. Er . . . we're doing what we can to play down the more sensational aspects, sir. There's a lot that doesn't need to come out – with your approval, that is.'

The policeman addressed this last surprising observation to Sir Archibald Rees, but his questioning expression as he got up to leave was firmly fixed on Treasure.

CHAPTER XXI

The Governor broke the momentary silence. 'You suspected Mrs Joyce? I don't see . . .'

Small's abrupt departure had been by prior arrangement. The banker felt less than comfortable about what was to follow, but it had been a considerable relief to the policeman that Treasure had volunteered to handle the most awkward aspect of the whole affair.

'I'd hoped very much we'd not have to suspect anyone of anything very serious.' Treasure let the words register before continuing. 'Until Small got the autopsy report it seemed highly probable that Joe O'Hara had died from a coronary – induced by the stress of his argument with Paul, followed by the climb to the cabin.'

'Exactly. I thought . . .' Rees hesitated and then made no effort to continue.

'Once we knew it was murder, and, in view of the means employed, a premeditated murder, Mrs Joyce was a pretty obvious candidate.'

'Not to me.'

'But you knew about her husband's relationship with another woman?'

Rees nodded: he looked embarrassed. 'That was a situation entirely –'

'Entirely governed by Joe O'Hara's intractable attitude to marriage,' Treasure interposed quietly. 'At least, so far as the top people on his island were concerned. The fact that the Joyces could never be divorced so long as Joe was alive must have been every bit as irksome to Mrs Joyce as

it was to her husband – and considerably more degrading.'
He paused. 'Freedom and dignity. Very strong motives, Sir
Archibald. Given that Mrs Joyce was aiming to recapture
both, she certainly had the means and the opportunity to
eliminate Joe. She must have been sure the cause of death
would be taken to be a heart attack – which it would, but
for the decapitation.'

Rees passed a shaking hand across his mouth. He made
as though to speak, then thought better of it.

Treasure was anxious to continue. 'The use of curarin
definitely pointed us towards Mrs Joyce – but not exclusively to her. She was a biochemist and had the
knowledge and facilities to make the stuff – but Small
proved last night that curarin wouldn't be difficult to
come by here in any case. No, it was the sophisticated
nature of the crime, plus the need for the murderer to
know Joe's whereabouts, that reduced the field of suspects.
Almost certainly it had to be someone at your dinner-party
on Thursday evening – and if it was, then Mrs Joyce was
the only one with a predetermined alibi.'

'Predetermined? How d'you mean?'

'As I said, she assumed there'd be no autopsy – but if
there was one she knew her husband would swear they'd
been together all night. He'd have to cover himself, and in
the process he'd be accounting for her. I doubt Chief
Ministers are very ready to admit to perjury. Mrs Joyce
was certain of it. She had a watertight alibi in advance,
vouched for by someone who'd have to assume it was true
without knowing whether it was or not.'

'But who'd never deny its validity. It was very astute
of you to deduce all that.' The Governor spoke without
emotion.

'It was very raw deduction, and highly theoretical. It
was Sarah's story that put us up to the idea of setting a
trap.'

'And risking a young life. Tempting the guilty into
committing a much more terrible crime.' This time
Rees's words were highly charged – almost venomously so.

'Not really,' Treasure answered lightly. 'You see, Sarah spent the night in my dressing-room – I hope you don't mind. And the trick worked, of course. Mrs Joyce panicked.' He shrugged his shoulders. 'It'd be charitable to think she went to Sarah's room with the idea of buying her silence – or even pleading for it.'

'But she was carrying a knife.'

'And a hypodermic charged with curarin. She didn't take her husband's hand-gun – according to Small, he has one – but there's no doubt she meant to kill the girl. She must have been convinced Sarah had seen her at the lodge. Of course, she hadn't.'

The Governor looked up with a jerk. 'Did Sarah see anyone at all?'

Treasure cupped his right hand in the palm of his left and appeared studiously to be examining his fingers. 'Around five-thirty she thought she saw a man she knew enter the lodge and a minute or two later place Joe O'Hara's head on the window ledge.' The banker looked up from his hands. Rees was sitting quite still, staring glassily into space. 'I believe O'Hara's – er – visitor arrived with the intention of offering him a ride to Mount Manitou on the footplate of a steam-engine, which he'd stopped on a test run ten minutes' walk away from the lodge – and which he subsequently drove back to Rupertstown arriving well within the time it would have taken to do the full round trip.'

Rees's head began to tremble, and he made as if to rise.

'Please stay where you are, Sir Archibald, and hear me out.' Treasure's tone was quiet but firm. 'I believe our well-intentioned caller quickly realized the cold body had been dead for some time, and that he naturally assumed the cause was a heart attack. I think he quickly and accurately calculated the effect of O'Hara's sudden death at this particular time – that the dynasty would continue, but led by someone he rightly considered unworthy. I believe he then – perhaps unwisely – surrendered to an urge to affect the course of events with a dramatic and

highly symbolic action. That action was suggested by the
date. It was made possible by the handy presence of a
machete, and it was arguably justified by the character of
Paul O'Hara.

'I think, also, our man was motivated not by impulse
but by a cool sense of opportunity – and there's a world of
difference. You see, he's neither impulsive nor irrespon-
sible by nature. For years, though, he's been seeking an
opportunity to help point this community in a new
direction – defensibly, towards an order more suited to
the times than paternalism or whatever form of un-
benevolent dictatorship Paul O'Hara could be expected to
dish out. In chopping off the head of the very dead Joe he
considered he was airing a very live issue – without hurt to
anyone.'

'Except himself. He was a bloody fool.' There was total
despair in the Governor's every syllable.

Treasure shrugged. 'He'd assumed he'd not been seen.
He knew his action would precipitate a post-mortem but
he relied on that proving Joe had long since died of a
coronary. It was reasonable to think the authorities would
soon tire of looking for the culprit. Oh, they'd go through
the motions but it would've been like looking for a needle
in a haystack.'

'Except for Sarah.' Again there was resignation in the
voice.

Treasure smiled. 'Sarah thought she'd identified Luke
Murphy in the half-light. She now knows it couldn't have
been Luke, and she's not chancing her arm at any other
guesses. She also knows she didn't witness a murder.'

'You mean . . . ?'

'I mean the detail of what Sarah thought she saw is
known to only four people besides herself – that's you, me,
my wife and Small. Since Sarah now chooses to believe it
never happened, the Chief Inspector would be glad if we'd
follow the same line.'

There was a ten-second silence; Treasure was counting.
When the Governor began to speak it was in the

dignified tone of a determined martyr. 'I appreciate Small's attitude – and the advice you have given him.' A flicker of a smile accompanied the last comment. 'However, foolish, precipitate action on my part –'

'Would be highly undesirable at the present time.' Treasure had interrupted without ceremony. 'What's needed is a cool show of firm leadership. Did you know Joyce is quitting the island for good?'

The Governor looked anything but cool, and far from firm. It was disarming to be stopped in mid-confession. 'He was here earlier to tell me as much. I tried to dissuade him, but he seems determined. He feels the situation here will be untenable for him.'

'And so it will.'

Rees shook his head solemnly. 'A strange man. I feel now I hardly know him.' Perplexity next gave way to disenchantment. 'He seemed untouched by the least sense of grief or guilt about his wife. He was preoccupied – outraged even – over his . . . his mistress's withdrawing from some financial commitment. A plan to finance the compulsory purchase of O'Hara Industries with her own money. I didn't quite understand . . .'

'Her own money or funds from the Franks-Barrett Trust?' Treasure began to fathom the reason that might lie behind the Chief Minister's earlier determination to remain on KCI.

'That was it. A family trust . . .'

'And a very rich one.' The banker nodded knowingly. 'But the trustees involved are quite as respectable as the Church Commissioners – and if anything, more fastidious. I doubt they'd extend their discretionary powers to back whatever eccentric scheme Joyce and Lady Cynthia may have in mind for KCI. Not in the present circumstances, anyway. The Trust tends to keep a low profile.' He smirked. 'It doesn't much go in for funding elaborate love-affairs – especially those subject to unexpected and un-desirable advertisement.'

Rees appeared to be ruminating rather than listening.

'I'd had such high hopes. Now it appears the island is doomed in every way.'

'Not at all.' Treasure was adamantly enthusiastic, and for not entirely altruistic reasons. 'One can't disguise the unpleasant nature of what's happened, but it's the future that matters. If you want my view, the O'Hara system couldn't have survived much longer – for a variety of reasons, and not all of them to do with marijuana. Joyce, on the other hand, and from what I've been told, wanted to move much too quickly – but some of his ideas were sound.'

The Governor looked like a small boy who had just been told his tricycle was not beyond repair. 'You see *any* future for us with Paul O'Hara controlling affairs?'

Treasure was touched and encouraged by his companion's evident identification with the community interest. 'A perfectly sound future – economically and constitutionally. Just as Joe O'Hara fancied himself as Charles the First, and came to a not dissimilar end' – Rees flinched – 'I think we might extend the analogy and have you moved into the William of Orange slot. Joyce has already quit as Cromwell, and somehow I don't see Paul O'Hara succeeding as Charles the Second or James the Second.'

Comprehension was visibly waning. 'I'm afraid . . .'

'I'm being too abstruse. Sorry, I was getting carried away – but you know there are aspects of this island's situation that . . .' Treasure shrugged and let the words tail off. It suddenly occurred to him that he had just cast Lady Rees in the substantial role of Queen Mary: historical analogy was rarely perfect. 'Given a month or so, I think you'll find things'll straighten out – but not by themselves. You're the key – ' he paused – 'your Excellency. And I think you know it.'

Sir Archibald Rees pondered for a moment, then slowly began to straighten in his chair.

It took rather longer than a month for a new and enduring

TREASURE UP IN SMOKE

order to be established on King Charles Island, but Treasure had been speaking figuratively. Nevertheless, the tranquillity and contentment that prevails there today more than proves his earliest expressed conviction.

In his capacity as Chief Magistrate, the Governor dismissed most of the charges against Paul O'Hara, and effectively ensured that none of them was transferred for hearing in a higher English Court.

O'Hara pleaded guilty inadvertently to burning down his house, thereby causing a nuisance and a great deal of public inconvenience and expense. His insistence that it had been a very ugly house was solemnly taken into account however, and the resulting fine was quite modest. In mitigation, the ruin – now covered in creeper – has a charm and character never possessed by the original building.

Since O'Hara made no claim against the insurance underwriters they could hardly charge him with attempting to defraud them, and sensibly accepted his deposition magnanimously excusing them from all liability in the matter. After deliberation, however, they pronounced they found themselves unable to meet his request to refund the unexpired part of the premium.

In consideration for this packaged and manipulated turn in events – and slightly in advance of its actual realization – O'Hara agreed to sell O'Hara Industries Ltd. to the newly formed King Charles Development Corporation at a price so low as to suggest his philanthropy bordered on insanity.

The Development Corporation – the brain-child of Mark Treasure – had no difficulty raising the loans to meet its very temporary obligations. The sums involved were modest, and quite quickly repaid after the organization's partnership enterprises with outside interests were formed and began to flourish.

The distillery has proved a modestly profitable venture, as has the yacht marina at Rupertstown and the exclusive villa, hotel and golf-club development at Roll-over Bay.

The much enlarged airport, while receiving only a strictly prescribed number of scheduled flights from Europe and the USA, specializes in the quartering and servicing of what with delicacy might be described as only the better class of private jet aeroplane – a seemly enough match for the type of vessels catered for at the marina.

Ignoring the views of five hundred relieved if inconvenienced Florida mountebanks, it came as no surprise that the previously scarce and sought after King Charles Elegantes enjoyed a singular success when offered in quantity to a wider market. Much enlarged and modernized production facilities led to allegedly staggering cost savings which were magnanimously passed on to the consumer. It was also averred that there had been no reduction in the quality of the tobaccos employed – a perfectly honest assertion; the tobaccos had always been indifferent and were now actually improved through the need to import additional supplies from Jamaica.

What underwrote the massive demand was the knowledge that a product previously within the reach of only the most affluent was now available to what in modern marketing terms is usually described as that distinguished (meaning large) group of smokers whose individual high discernment and impeccable good taste far outmatches their modest incomes. This assertion was objectively reinforced – in part, perhaps, even suggested – by an equally discerning and tasteful international advertising campaign.

While the Sunfun Hotel Corporation of America did not feature as principals in any of these successful ventures, Glen Dogwall and his attractive wife are frequent visitors to their villa on the island where they repair to get away from the people who frequent the kind of resorts where the Sunfun Hotel Corporation of America do feature as principals. Although it was initially a source of irritation to Mr Dogwall that Sunfun obtained no concessions on the island, it became a growing source of satisfaction to him that Mongo Joyce enjoyed none either.

As for the ex-Chief Minister's own career since leaving KCI, this is too well known to need recounting in detail. Following the latest judgement by the International Court at the Hague, it now seems unlikely that the Shetland island purchased by Joyce's second wife, and which the two have made their home, will be permitted either to secede from the United Kingdom or to be invested with the North Sea oil revenues the owners have claimed belong to their domain.

Father Aloysius Babington came gradually to accept the new order of things, as did Angus McLush who, although deprived of his income as a spy and conscious that he had somehow let a scoop slip through his fingers, was formally appointed Chief Information Officer to the Development Corporation. It has not been in his nature to cavil that he is the only Information Officer.

Through the intervention of Molly Treasure, Sarah Rafferty achieved her ambition to train as a nurse in London – an arrangement very much approved by Sir Archibald Rees who was glad to have her fully occupied some distance away from KCI. Apart from other considerations, this avoided the girl being tempted to return to purposeless speculation on who it might have been whom she saw serving up the head of Joe O'Hara on that fateful morning – and through her daily proximity to Government House possibly arriving at the right conclusion.

The Governor continues to be regarded as a model colonial administrator – so much so that it is sometimes regretted by older heads at the Foreign Office that, due to the acute shortage of colonies, there is little opportunity left for his exemplary performance to be emulated. For his own part, it is reward enough that the British Government met the cost of salvaging and refitting the indestructible *Sir Dafydd*, now once more the soundest and oldest narrow-gauge steam-engine in working order west of Talyllyn.

The burgeoning romance between Debby Rees and Peregrine Gore is a fitful affair. Despite the warmth of their correspondence before Debby arrived in Britain en route for Cambridge, the path of true love took a swerve when he met her at London Airport and drove her at high speed to Oxford: they are still good friends.

The Treasures visit KCI from time to time as the guests of the Governor. Most recently Treasure has tried to ensure that such trips coincide with the presence on the island of a Harley Street surgeon friend who bought a villa there. Such precaution he considers prudent following a stomach-ache which was first wrongly diagnosed as a grumbling appendix: one cannot be too careful about such things. Molly simply checks before leaving that there is a bottle of antacid tablets in her make-up case.

Lord Grenwood continues to be immoderately pleased with the way Treasure handled the KCI situation – on his behalf. He also takes credit for somehow having sensed Archie Rees's true potential from the very start – as well as Peregrine's underestimated acuity. How many young bankers these days, he once enquired, could be called upon to start a steam-engine? Although the question was clearly rhetorical, Treasure, to whom it was addressed, registered the rueful reply that he guessed the number was marginally greater than those who could be relied upon to stop one.

It was during this same conversation that Grenwood had summoned his secretary – name of Caroline – to find him a fresh box of Punch Havana cigars. He did not much care for the King Charles Elegantes kept on his desk for offering to less important visitors.

'Can't see why people rave about those stinkers, Mark,' he observed. 'Considering our interest, wouldn't mention it to anyone else of course, but if you ask me they're only fit for . . . for . . . burning. What!'

While his lordship surrendered to the uncontrollable mirth engendered by his quip, Treasure, though agreeing with the sentiment, silently steeled himself to resist inviting Sister Helena to suggest ways of improving the product.